Wonderful
Girl

Wonderful Girl

BY AIMEE LaBRIE

2007 WINNER, KATHERINE ANNE PORTER PRIZE IN SHORT FICTION

University of North Texas Press
Denton, Texas

10 9 8 7 6 5 4 3 2 1

Permissions:
University of North Texas Press
P.O. Box 311336
Denton, TX 76203-1336

The paper used in this book meets the minimum requirements of the American National Standard for Permanence of Paper for Printed Library Materials, z39.48.1984. Binding materials have been chosen for durability.

Library of Congress Cataloging-in-Publication Data
LaBrie, Aimee, 1969–
  Wonderful girl / by Aimee LaBrie.
      p. cm.
  "2007 Winner, Katherine Anne Porter Prize in Short Fiction."
  ISBN 978-1-57441-240-6 (pbk. : alk. paper)
  1. Young women—Fiction. I. Title.
  PS3612.A278W66 2007
  813'.6—dc22
                                    2007027204

Wonderful Girl is Number 6 in the Katherine Anne Porter Prize in Short Fiction Series

This is a work of fiction. Any resemblance to actual events or establishments or to persons living or dead is unintentional.

Text design by Carol Sawyer/Rose Design

To Donna and Lurye

Contents

Acknowledgments

"Ducklings" was previously published in *Pleiades* and was nominated for a Pushcart Prize.

"Wanted" was published in *The Cimarron Review*.

"In Mem" was published in *Passages North*.

"Our Last Supper" was published as "Visitation" in *Scribner's Best of the Fiction Workshop, 1998* and Spelunker *Flophouse*.

"Wonderful Girl" was published by *Philadelphia Stories* magazine and will be published in their up-coming anthology.

"What She Should Do" was published (under another title) in *The Minnesota Review*.

"The Last Dead Boyfriend" was published in *Eclipse*.

"Signs" was published in *Writer to Writer*.

"Look at the Sky and Tell me What You See" was published as "Dressing the Part" in *Strong Coffee and Permafrost*.

"Words to Live By" was published by *Exquisite Corpse*.

"Encore" appeared in *Sudden Stories: A Mammoth Anthology of Minuscule-Fiction* and *Quarter After Eight*.

"Another Cancer Story" was published in *Beloit Fiction Journal*.

"Snowball" was published in *Iron Horse Literary Review*.

"Six Different Ways . . ." was a finalist in the *Central PA Magazine* short story contest.

Ducklings

arjorie just loves babies! By the time she is twenty, she is going to have four: two girls and two boys. The girls will be identical twins, but she won't be the type of mother who makes them wear matching dresses with white pinafores. Marjorie is well aware of the importance of individuality! She will have their eyes checked routinely. If they are anything like her, they'll need Coke-bottle glasses before they are five years old!

She hangs posters around the neighborhood telephone poles: "Responsible Girl Available for Sitting. Prices may vary." The last line is especially good, because that way, she can ask for more money, if the parents have three kids of varying ages. It isn't wise to become enslaved by a stranger.

Marjorie is twelve, but she is not a child. For one thing, instead of Judy Blume young adult novels, she checks out Betty

Crocker recipe books, home decorating manuals, and self-help paperbacks like *If I'm so Wonderful, Why Am I Still Single?* She slices her mother's grapefruit for breakfast, suggests baths with Epsom salt when Mom's eyelids sag, and dyes Mom's hair with L'Oreal burnt auburn every three months, exclaiming, "You look almost as good as new!"

The posters work like a charm. Mrs. Langly from church calls to ask if Marjorie can baby-sit on Friday. Her two regular sitters have the stomach flu. "This Friday?" Marjorie taps a pencil against her forehead. "Hold just one second, please." She pinches the roll of fat overlapping her skirt and mouths "Pig-face" at her wavy reflection in the toaster. She returns to the phone. "This Friday sounds perfect."

Mrs. Langly's breath rushes out. "Is everything okay?" Marjorie asks with what she hopes sounds like concern. She doesn't really want to know the answer, but these are the kinds of questions you are supposed to ask.

A lighter clicks. Is Mrs. Langly having a cigarette? Does she do that around the baby? Doesn't she know how bad second-hand smoke is? "My husband—Bill—has to have emergency surgery. My mother's flying in Saturday to stay with us, so . . ."

Marjorie's face turns hot. She has seen Mr. Langly in church belting out "Amazing Grace" in a way that is embarrassing. She vaguely remembers a thick head of hair and bushy eyebrows and maybe a handlebar moustache. Marjorie pictures the doctors in the ER working on his Adam's apple. "Awww . . ." she says, a drawn-out, fake noise like you make when someone tells a bad joke. It is the wrong sound. Perhaps it is not the best time to discuss the hourly rate. "Babies are kind of a hobby of mine." Mrs. Langley says nothing. "So, yes, siree! I'll be there with bells on!"

Jeopardy blares from the black-and-white TV propped on a dinner tray. "Mom? I won't be around on Friday. I have a job."

"Okay." Marjorie's mother lies in bed, squinting at a picture of a skinny model in an entertainment magazine.

Marjorie switches on the lamp. "Do you need anything?"

Marjorie's mother shields her eyes like a person coming out of a tunnel. "No. I'll make dinner in a while."

Marjorie heats up the Lean Cuisines. What if Mr. Langly bleeds to death and Mrs. Langly is so upset, she crashes her car and then, the grandmother blows to bits in a plane crash on the way to claim the baby? Everyone knows bad luck comes in threes. Marjorie would have to take care of him on her own. She still has her doll crib and that would do until he gets older. She would go to school with purple circles under her eyes, smiling weakly at the teachers when she handed in her assignments, all turned in on time, but with yellow baby-food fingerprints along the bottom. Her English teacher, Mr. Moon, might pull her aside and wrestle the story out of her. Mr. Moon has a soft voice, a football-sized potbelly, and large, light blue eyes that penetrate the soul. Once he discovered Marjorie's plight, he would say, "Brave girl," putting his chalky hands on her face and kissing her, maybe whispering into her hair words from an Ogden Nash poem. She turned in a paper about "The Duck," and Mr. Moon gave her C+ and wrote "Interesting Ideas!" in blue pen on the bottom.

Marjorie has 101 interesting ideas.

The night before the job, Marjorie can't sleep. Her brain keeps popping up with possible accidents that could occur. She trips on a squeaky toy while carrying the baby and he flies out of her arms and impales himself on scissors. She forgets to lay him down the right way in the crib and he suffocates on a stuffed giraffe. She turns on the oven and the house blows to smithereens.

To distract herself, Marjorie begins making up names for the baby, starting with the letter "M."

On Friday, Marjorie puts on a white button-up shirt and plaid skirt. The skirt is too tight and the buttons don't meet, so she fastens it closed with a safety pin. She and her mother have been on a diet. They eat half a piece of fruit for breakfast, a shake for lunch, and a diet frozen dinner at night. Marjorie's mother is as fat as ever. When Marjorie looks at her, she sees what she could become.

Before she leaves to baby-sit, she tells her mother that she's left the Langlys' number next to a list of what's for dinner under the smiley face magnet on the fridge. "Have a good time," her mother says, turning the TV channels rapidly, each station a blur of noise and brightness.

Marjorie is almost to the Langlys' when three greasy-haired boys from school turn the corner in front of her. She considers cutting across a yard, but one of them spots her, and they start trailing after her on their stupid, too small dirt bikes. "Where you going, Marjorie?" They always pretend to be nice at first.

Marjorie tugs at the hem of her skirt. "Baby-sitting." It's best not to let them know they are getting under your skin. When they throw spitballs at her on the bus, Marjorie lets the wads collect in her hair. She never turns around. At school, she picks the spitballs out and drops them into the toilet, imagining each circle is one of their heads, so when she flushes, she can watch them drown in the bowl.

"Hey, Large Marge!" they call. "Margarine!" Marjorie stares straight ahead, trying not to listen to her thighs rubbing together as she walks. They are just adolescents. She has a womanly figure, and they can't help ogling, because their penises keep clouding their brains. She learned that from her mother. Hopefully, they will die soon and leave her alone.

"Baby-sitting! We've got something for you to sit on!" Ralph has a round, Jack-o-lantern face. "Hey, let's see your award, Margarine!"

He is referring to the Pride Award she won last month for her essay titled, "How I Helped My Mother Through a Difficult Time." The difficult time Marjorie wrote about was how she studied with her mother to help her memorize the medical terminology for her nurses' licensing exam after Marjorie's father ran off. She wrote about how her mother took night classes for many months and how Marjorie was left at home alone and had to fend for herself.

One time, Marjorie asked, "Does this mean you won't be home to make dinner?" Her mother began weeping, making large whooping noises while Marjorie shifted from one foot to the other, silently repeating, Stupid, stupid, stupid. She didn't mention this particular moment in her essay. The other part she left out was the miscarriage.

When Marjorie first heard the word, she imagined a baby carriage tumbling over, like, whoops, missed the carriage! But it is more complicated than that. First of all, she hadn't even known her mother was pregnant! The essay did not describe how Marjorie helped her mother into the bathroom and held her while she threw up, and how she mopped up the tile afterwards with a Squeegee. It was a lot of blood! Marjorie pretended she was on a game show. The faster she scrubbed the blood off the floor, the bigger the prize—a car, a horse, a new house.

Ralph skids his bike in the gravel, throwing a spray of stones against Marjorie's legs. "Hey, Marge, aren't the parents afraid you'll eat the baby?" The other boys snort and pop wheelies.

Marjorie has thought many times what to do in emergency situations. For instance, don't look a rabid German Shepherd in the eye. She runs as fast as she can (not very), up the sidewalk and to Mrs. Langly's door, waiting for one of them to chase after her, grab her by the neck, and pull her into the bushes. But when she glances back, they have disappeared.

She will make a good impression. She will not do anything dumb.

Mrs. Langly answers the doorbell right away. Her smile wavers. Marjorie holds out her hand. "Good afternoon. I am the baby-sitter, Marjorie."

Mrs. Langly shakes Marjorie's hand. "Oh."

The baby blubbers from behind her. "Da, Da, Da."

"My mother taught me how to do baby CPR." This is untrue, but she has seen a diagram. Mrs. Langly is a professional woman. Scarecrow thin, chin-length blond hair, lipstick with liner, a black blouse, neatly pleated gray pants and tiny pearl earrings. "I just love those."

Mrs. Langly's manicured fingernails fly to her ear. "Oh, these. Bill gave them to me for our tenth anniversary."

"My mom has that same outfit," she lies again.

"That's nice." Mrs. Langly checks her watch. "Come in and meet the baby." Marjorie follows her through the door. "The only place we don't allow him is my husband's office. He knows better. He's a good baby." The baby, as if aware he is being discussed, toddles around the corner encased in a baby bumper car, fat legs propelling him across the floor.

"How darling!" Marjorie dislikes the baby immediately. His dark eyes press into his face like raisins, his cheeks puff out, and his arms and legs are doughy, white rolls. He is a gigantic, snowman-shaped Christmas cookie.

"He weighs more at ten months than I did by age one!" Mrs. Langly claps at the baby. "Don't you, chubba-hubbah?" The baby sticks out a fat purple lip. "We love him anyway." Mrs. Langly laughs.

She gives Marjorie a quick tour the house ending with the nursery. The baby's bedroom glows in hushed whites and blues, cozy and dark. It smells like Lysol and poop. Little yellow ducks waddle across the top of the wall and the crib is full to bursting with stuffed animals. Marjorie makes a mental note to take those out before the baby goes to sleep so he won't suffocate.

While Mrs. Langly explains the rules, Marjorie answers, "Right. I see. 10–4," hearing her words like a voice at the end of a bad phone connection. How would it feel to live in this house with Mr. Langly for a husband? Marjorie is dying to find a picture of him. She keeps getting him confused in her mind with a movie actor who wears a moustache. She must know if Mr. Langly has one. If he does, she is in danger of falling instantly in love.

Mrs. Langly winds down and looks at the baby (Is the baby's name Sammy? Stanley? Would they really name the baby Stanley Langly?). "Be a good boy," she tells him. She swivels on her heel to face Marjorie. "I left the number for St. Joseph's Hospital on the refrigerator. In case of anything." Mrs. Langly rearranges the fruit magnets on the icebox: pineapple, apple, banana. "I won't be gone long."

"The baby and I are going to have a splendid time!" Marjorie smiles like she does for school photos, holding the grin longer than is comfortable. The baby glances from Marjorie to his mother, a string of saliva dribbling down his double chin. "Say, 'So long, Mommy.'" The baby whimpers, holding his hands up to his mother.

Mrs. Langly gives him an elephant-shaped animal cracker. "You two stay out of trouble." As soon as she leaves, Marjorie locks the front door.

She waits until the car pulls out of the driveway. Then she leans over the baby. He wears a sky blue jumper with white felt rabbits hopping across the front. She touches his crown, searching for the soft spot on him like on a melon. The baby turns his head in her hands, trying to look at her. "I'm going to eat you up." She puts her nose to the crook of his neck and inhales: sour milk and baby powder. "Don't make me put you in the microwave."

Marjorie checks the closets (no fur coat, but two London Fog jackets side by side, baby stroller, vacuum cleaner). She runs her fingers across the CDs, the leather books on the shelves, the silk lilies in a crystal vase on the dining room table. The baby trails after her, his toes grazing the carpet as he lurches and bounces like a pinball against the coffee table, the end table, and the velveteen chairs. Will he tell his parents years later, "Remember that fat girl? She snooped as soon as you left."

"I'm just taking inventory," she sprints away from the baby and ducks into the office.

The room is dark, windowless, with a stale smell of burnt coffee and tobacco smoke. There is a mahogany desk with a calendar, the squares marked up with red pen in Mr. Langly's neat, slanted handwriting. Marjorie traces her finger over the writing. Books, notes, and stacks of paper are arranged purposefully, like in a library. Marjorie picks up a page, reads. "New link between Melville and Hemingway? See Lydia for info." Who is Lydia? His lover? The former baby-sitter?

She pulls down her shirtsleeve to open the desk drawers. She finds pens, paper clips, more notes, and a maroon bankbook. They have $10,342.45 in their savings account. Can that be right? If Mrs. Langly dies, maybe Mr. Langly will marry Marjorie. She could nurse him through his mourning, and he might confess he never really loved his wife. The baby would forget all about his real mother and come to love Marjorie instead, and Marjorie could send her mother to Hawaii.

The baby stands in his carrier on the edge of the office with a tsk-tsk look on his face. "Come on in, baby. It's okay." The baby takes a wobbling step forward. "No!" she says. He jerks back. "It's okay," she says again, gently, but the baby won't move. She pats her knees as if she is calling a dog. "It's okay. It's okay." The baby starts toward her again and Marjorie yells, "No!" The baby starts crying. Marjorie lifts him out of the carrier. "I'm sorry. It's okay, you're a good boy."

She heaves the baby unto her hip like she's seen mothers on TV do. The baby is unwieldy and heavy. He keeps wiggling and whining in her ear like a mosquito. "I'm your mother now," she tells him. Also, "There is no Santa Claus." The baby burps. "Your father might die," she says, although she knows this probably isn't true. The baby's head swivels back and forth, and he tries to touch everything they come close to.

Marjorie takes him to the stove to teach him an important rule in safety. The baby reaches forward. "No, no, baby, see it's hot." She puts her hand on the burner and shakes it. "Ouch! You can get third-degree burns if you're not careful." The baby gurgles wetly, so she does it a few more times, until she starts to feel like he is manipulating her into acting like an idiot.

"Let's see what's in the bedroom," she jostles the baby up and down like a sack of flour. "Bedroom. Bedroom." The Langlys' bedroom has vacuum cleaner marks on the shag carpet and a king-sized bed in the center with a floral, puffy bedspread. Marjorie plops the baby in the center of the bed. "Stay." He flops on his back and stares at the ceiling fan. Marjorie's footsteps leave heavy dark imprints on the thick carpeting. She must vacuum when she's done. "Remind me, Baby."

A long, sleek dresser with a gilt-edged mirror reflects the room, mostly the bed. That's so they can look at each other. She opens a drawer. Mrs. Langly wears silk underwear with lace. Her bras are size 34-B, two sizes smaller than Marjorie's. Mr. Langly's underwear waits in the next drawer: white Fruit of the Loom folded neatly, crotch over the waistband. His actual penis has been on this cloth. Marjorie touches the top pair with her index finger, feeling light-headed.

In the nightstand drawer are three Polaroid pictures. The first one is Mr. and Mrs. Langly, sprawled naked on the bedspread together. Mr. Langly has the camera held out at arm's length, showing a bare chest with a matted knot of dark, gorilla hair and pink nipples. No moustache. His smile is huge and cartoonish. The other picture shows Mrs. Langly in a red teddy, her head cocked to the side as if she has just heard the distant chime of a bell. In the last photo, Mr. Langly stands completely nude, holding his thing in his hand and smiling at the camera. Marjorie cannot believe it! Mr. Langly's penis. She can't get the phrase out of her mind. It's like having water in your ear. They actually do it in this exact same bed. "Don't look, Baby." The baby bicycles his legs in the air.

Marjorie must check how the baby's penis compares. She unsnaps the jumper, pulls back the stickies, and whips off the diaper. The baby's penis is a tiny thumb, Mr. Langly's more like a paper towel roll. The baby fixes his black eyes on her. "What?" She tickles his stomach and pee shoots straight into the air, splashing Marjorie's hand.

Marjorie runs to the bathroom to get a Kleenex. She pauses to look inside the mirrored medicine cabinet and finds: Dr. Scholl's foot powder, a make-up bag, extra toilet paper, super-absorbency tampons, a douche, hot rollers, soap and shampoo from Holiday Inn.

There is a muffled thump followed by a mournful wail. Marjorie drops the soap and streaks back to the bedroom.

The baby has landed face first on the rug. He waves his arms and legs, wiggling like a turtle. When she picks him up, she sees a red bump swelling in the center of his forehead. She carries him into his bedroom and sets him on the diaper-changer. He squawks. Marjorie grabs the Johnson's baby powder and squeezes it in the middle. "Look, baby, look!" The baby stops crying to watch the powder whoosh and fall in to the floor. "See there? Snowflakes! It's Christmastime!"

She squeezes until the powder is almost gone, and the baby shows his gums, the red welt a shiny cherry on his forehead. She could put a Band-Aid on it, but maybe the bump should be allowed to breathe. She carries the baby into the Langlys' bathroom and rummages around the cabinet under the sink. She finds Mrs. Langly's flowered make-up bag and applies a thin coat of Max Factor foundation over the lump. "You're a movie star!" She holds the baby up to the mirror by his armpits. His legs buckle and straighten, buckle and straighten, as if he were a marionette. She adds a circle of blush. When she's finished, he has been transformed into a dwarf baby from *The Wizard of Oz*. After the welt goes down, she will wash his face and put on Bactine in case of infection. Until then, he'll just have to be glamorous.

The phone rings. Marjorie jogs with the baby to the kitchen. "The Langlys!" Silence. "Hello? Hello?"

"Hey, Margarine!" She hangs up. It rings again. "Can we come over, Margie?" She slams the receiver down and then picks it up, unplugging the phone cord from the socket.

Marjorie fits the baby into his highchair. In the cupboards are: Triscuits, Wheaties, Nutri-Grain bars, pasta. The inside drawers of the refrigerator are crammed with celery, fresh red apples, and a head of lettuce. Jars of Gerbers march across the shelves, the faces lined up in a row like a miniature baby army. Marjorie shakes one called "Plum Dessert." The baby reaches out, fingers splayed like a starfish.

"Plum Dessert" tastes a little like plums, a lot like water. The baby jiggles up and down in his highchair and hits his hands on the tray. "You want some?" Marjorie airplanes the spoon through the air. The baby darts forward, taking the spoon down his throat. He gags. "Whoops," Marjorie pats his back. When people really choke, they cannot cough or speak. "Good boy." The baby howls and his arm flies out, knocking the jar out of Marjorie's hands. It crashes, but doesn't break, splattering purple juice across the white tile floor. "Damnit to hell." This is what Marjorie's mother says when things go wrong. Marjorie has never sworn before, but it feels right, fitting. "Damnit. Damnit. Damnit."

She takes the screaming baby into the living room. Her arms and legs feel numb, but the clock over the mantel tells her she has only been there for half an hour. Time certainly does not fly!

A figure glides by the front window. Marjorie freezes. Another someone runs past and ducks behind the bushes. She cannot think what to do. What's the number for the police? She should know this, but really, she is stupid. She tiptoes to the front door. Dirt bikes sprawl across the front lawn. A knock on the window, followed by a low laugh. Marjorie can feel her heart in her chest. Such rapid heartbeats can signal what's known as a myocardial infarction. The baby wants down, but she clutches him to her chest. He wails loud enough for the neighbors to hear and call the police. "Shush, shush, shush," she tells him, but his skin moves between crimson and white, tears and snot streaming down his face. The foundation runs down the baby's face, causing a splattering of tiny red dots to appear, probably an allergy to the make-up. "Be quiet. Please, I beg of you!" She crouches by the sofa, the baby tucked under her arm.

"Mmm!" the baby blubbers. "Ma-mmm!"

A car splashes through a puddle and Marjorie hears it slow in front of the Langlys' yard, then a horn honks and deep-voice bellows, "Get out of there!" The boys scatter like birds from the bushes. One of them stops long enough to lob a tomato at the window, and it splats bright red across the glass.

Marjorie carries the baby to the living room mirror. "Look, look, who's that naughty baby crying for no reason?" Marjorie's ponytail has fallen down and purple juice dots her white shirt and glasses. She is so ugly, and the baby is so ugly, and the baby hates her. He pushes away from her chest with hard fingers as though she is a monster. "That's enough!" She won't hit the baby, because the Langlys would just be the kind of people to keep a hidden camera on the bookshelf. Marjorie grabs the baby carrier and tries to stick him into it. He kicks and squirms, so she jams him inside. He screams even louder, a high-pitched, keening, baby-murdering noise. "Shut up!" She yanks his foot through the holes. The baby lays his head on the tray, sobbing. Marjorie feels tears rise in her throat. "Quit being so melodramatic," she tells the baby, but he continues wailing like someone at a funeral.

A drop of sweat slides down Marjorie's arm. She drags the baby carrier across the room. "Here, baby. I'll let you go into the office." The baby picks his head up, as though he understands her. "You want the office?" His eyes widen and he shakes his head. "It's okay, I'll let you go in. Just don't tell your mommy." The baby moans. "What?" Marjorie drags the carrier toward the door. The baby hiccups and starts crying again, holding his hands up to Marjorie, which makes Marjorie feel like sobbing too. "Why don't you want to go in there?" Marjorie pushes the baby across the office. The baby bellows again, and tries to turn around. She leaves him in the middle of the floor, surrounded by papers and books. "Everything is okay!" she yells through the shut door, feeling a hard knot of shame in her stomach.

Things to do: Vacuum, mop, wash front window, baby needs a bath, get him in his nightclothes, dinner. She lies on the sofa, turning the volume up on the TV until the baby crying is a faint echo.

Marjorie dreams of babies—all in little white bonnets with round, fat faces. They waddle and quack through a grassy meadow. Her job is to keep them from toddling off a nearby cliff into the

Atlantic Ocean, but there are too many. They pop out of the ground faster than dandelions. She sits one down, and three more lumber off in different directions. The waves hitting the rocks below make a musical crash, luring the babies to the edge like the Pied Piper.

Mrs. Langly stands over her. At first, Marjorie hopes that this is part of the dream. No, Mrs. Langly is real, although her suit jacket is wrinkled and black smudges of mascara ring her eyes. She shakes Marjorie. "Where is the baby?" She searches behind chairs and under the sofa. Marjorie points to the office.

Mrs. Langly returns with the baby over her shoulder, knocked out cold in a deep sleep. "How did he get in that room? Get up." She pulls Marjorie by her arm into the office.

The book stacks have toppled, and Mr. Langly's papers fan across the carpet like big pieces of confetti. "Do you see this?" Yes, she sees. Marjorie straightens a book splayed flat on the ground, *The Canonization of Moby Dick.*

Mrs. Langly darts into the living room, where she perches on the edge of the sofa, rocking the baby too fast. "I cannot believe this. I tried calling you. Who were you on the phone with for so long?" Mrs. Langly has a flat, shiny look in her eyes like a person who has been in an accident. The medical terminology for this condition is "doll's eyes." It was on her mother's test.

"Do you want me to fix you some tea?" Marjorie asks. Mrs. Langly holds onto the baby like he's a life preserver. Something bad has happened to Mr. Langly. Worse than running off with Lydia. "Tea coming right up!"

"I don't believe it." Mrs. Langly's cheek twitches. "I don't."

Marjorie goes into the kitchen. She uses paper towels to mop up the plum juice from the floor. She takes a blue coffee mug from the cupboard. Blue is a soothing color. It can actually lower your blood pressure by two points. She drops a cinnamon apple teabag into the blue mug. When the teakettle whistles, Marjorie will fill the cup three quarters full, adding a little cold water from the tap so Mrs. Langley won't burn her mouth. She will put the cup on a saucer and add a little honey to make it sweet. She will sit by Mrs. Langley while she drinks her cup of tea.

This, after all, is something she knows how to do.

Another Cancer Story

*M*y younger sister Molly calls, interrupting my bedtime ritual of red wine and Marlboro lights (My friend Toby always asks, How can you smoke when your mother is dying of cancer? I answer, How can you not?). I check the clock. One a.m. No matter how many late night phone calls I get from Molly, the adrenaline rush of fear still clogs my throat.

Molly knows this feeling. She says, "Don't worry, JoAnne. Mom hasn't keeled over." Since we've been in this dying business together for so long, my sister is allowed to say whatever she wants. Keeled over, carried out feet first, bitten the big one. We have made up our own sayings for death: gone to the raspberry patch, hatched the last egg, galloped to Bethlehem. This is one of the ways we manage not to kick the bucket ourselves.

I ask Molly, "How close to buying the farm is she?"

Molly will be in the kitchen, hunched over with her ankles crossed under the table and speaking with her hand over the receiver like a Russian spy. Mom waits in the living room, where the hospital bed has landed like a giant spacecraft. The TV will be tuned to Channel 52, the all-Spanish network which plays Spanish-speaking soap operas, weather reports, and game shows. When she still had a sense of humor, Mom explained her rationale for watching. "This is my last chance to learn another language."

Molly calls me back to Earth. "Jack just left." Jack is the Hospice worker we love and who always brings us mint chocolate chip ice cream and Mom Dr. Pepper with a straw. He has been coming to Mom's house for two years now. He will stand in the living room, shaking his big lovely head like he can't take it anymore. Most people have Hospice care during the last two months of their expected life span. Mom has that record beat twelve times over. She remains a wonder of nature, like a two-headed calf or Siamese twins. Molly continues, "Jack gave me the 'What to do the week before your loved one's death' hand-out." We received the "What to do in two weeks" pamphlet four months ago. Molly and I have been thinking about writing one called, "What to do when your loved one won't die."

I don't know what to tell Molly. The clock over the sink tick-tocks in time to the dripping faucet. Since Mom was diagnosed, everything (especially clocks, calendars) has taken on this weighty significance, like the thump under the floorboards in Poe's "The Tell-Tale Heart."

"JoAnne." She enunciates her words carefully, as though speaking to a foreign exchange student. "I need you here."

"Si." I say. "Yo comprendo."

I drive Mom's old Buick from Chicago to Kankakee, land of the strip malls, garbage dumps, and late-night taco joints. How many times have I made this trip this year alone? I press the car pedal down for each number—six, seven, eight. How many days have I missed work? My boss with the unending cold suspects Mom is a creation of mine, like the dead grandparent excuse you use in college when you've missed a test. At first, she was sympathetic, but now when I tell her I need a few days away, she clenches her jaw and chirps, "How awful for you!"

When I arrive at Mom's, the dog jumps up on my knees and then rolls over. I scratch his stomach until his back leg churns. "Hey, Fat-head." I put my nose against his black and white Holstein cow fur, breathing in his dusty dog smell. He tucks his head in my armpit.

The house smells of Lysol, rubber gloves and a subtle, cloying scent that leaves a taste like a copper penny in your mouth.

Molly trudges into the foyer. Even though she's twenty-three, she's trapped in the flat body of an adolescent. She tugs at my jacket. "You missed the vomiting of the vanilla pudding extravaganza." Molly has chopped her dark brown hair into a short, practical bob so it won't get in the way of her bedside manner. She blinks her long eyelashes, flirting with me because I've shown up again. She is so cute that I want to put her in my pocket.

In the living room, a night-light shines by the television—the Virgin Mary with her blue gown, hands folded, and eyes raised toward the ceiling. Mom asked us to put the Virgin within her eyesight a few months ago to remind her that she hates God.

On a foldout tray: a water jug, a covered bedpan, Mom's eyeglasses, a green washcloth, a copy of Stephen King's *Pet Sematary*. Pill vials of Dramamine for nausea, Ativan for anxiety, Tylenol, and Percodan for fun. The Percodan makes her woozy, knocked-out loopy; she starts thinking Molly and I are South American kidnappers.

Today, Mom wears the yellow silk pajamas I bought her at Marshall Fields and a blue bandana tied pirate style. When she spots me, her hands flutter to her head. You have to approach her like a rescue worker calming a treed cat. "It's okay. It's okay."

She cries for a few minutes because she doesn't know who I am. Then she sits up shrewdly, as if she has been playing a role in a mini-drama and weren't we fooled? "Look out, Watson," she says.

I say, "I will." She coughs for a long, long time, eyes wide. I rub her back. The hard bony ridges of her spine and the hollows of her cheekbones are so familiar now that I can't remember what she used to look like. Sometimes, I have to search through old photo albums to remember her solid plump Mom body and wavy brown hair, the person she used to be.

"Where am I? Where am I?" She repeats this again and again until my sister brings her a framed picture of Molly and me standing in front of the house wearing the awful Pepto Bismol pink dresses Mom made us one Easter.

"Here is where you are." Molly points to the picture and then to the window. "See? There's your shrub that you like. You're at 412 Merriweather Lane. Your favorite place in the world."

"I bet," she says, but she sits back, her head lolling on her neck like a heavy bowling ball.

Molly tucks the blanket around Mom's thick red socks. I arrange her pill bottles alphabetically before asking, "Does she even know what day it is?"

Mom snaps awake. "It's Thursday. I may have cancer," she says. "But I'm not deaf." This is what makes it the hardest. She's still in there somewhere.

She told us early on what she doesn't want after she's dead: "No morbid organ playing 'Amazing Grace.' No 'Rage, rage against the dying of the light' or sentimental rhymes or obituary pictures of me in the newspaper wearing pearls with 'Sadly Missed' or 'Our Dear Departed Mother,' under my high school yearbook photo. I want a no-nonsense tombstone next to your father without an angel's head carved on it."

A year ago, she picked out her own coffin. Her face had thinned, but she still looked mostly like herself. She leaned against my arm, and we snail-crawled across the blue plush carpet of Fred Lyle's Mortuary. The undertaker rushed forward on silent pointy-toed shoes. He looked the part, pale and ghoulish—as though he had just stepped away from a remake of *Night of the Living Dead*. After we shook his sweaty, solemn hand, Mom asked him if she could test-drive one of the coffins.

"Excuse me?" He cocked his pointy ear at Mom.

She gave him her Southern girl smile. "Do you mind if I climb in this green casket? I want to see how it feels."

He didn't find us funny at all.

Now, the same undertaker calls to ask how she's doing, meaning is she dead yet? I tell him that she's made a full recovery and joined the Ice Capades.

He clears his throat. "I'm sorry?"

I say, "I'm sorry too." He starts to speak. "But we'll be sure to keep you in mind for the next family tragedy." I hang up without saying good-bye. At a certain point, you stop caring what people think. Especially the ones who assume she's died because, dear God, how could she be hanging on after all this time?

Eight months ago, she insisted on divvying up the things in the house. "JoAnne, you'll get the flower stickies on the bottom of the tub. Molly, I will you my jar of buttons. Everything else goes to Mothers Against Drunk Driving." Molly and I turned our mouths up in an attempt to be smiling. Mom sighed as though she was tired of us not recognizing her. "Who wants the sewing machine?" The whir of her machine was the main sound effect of our childhood. When Molly and I didn't respond, she said. "We'll sell it to the nuns then."

"No!" Molly and I said together.

Finally, she asked, "What do you girls really want?"

Molly raised her hand. "The toaster oven."

"Your watch." I answered before Molly could think of it.

The watch has a thin silver band, a small round face with Roman numerals, and a loud tick. It is the sound I heard every time I stayed home from school with a fever, her cool palm on my forehead, smelling of Lemon Fresh Joy, the sound of her watch in my ear. Most times, she pronounced me healed, and most times, she was right.

"You win." Mom said. She unfastened her watch and handed it to me, leaving a clean white band of skin on her wrist.

Molly and I take her Percodan. Everything blisses out blue and yellow, fuzzy around the edges. Molly has a halo. Mom is an angel in silk pajamas. This is nice, I think. It's not so bad after all. But then my legs fill with cement and my throat thickens. I struggle to stand up from the sofa. Everything feels cocooned in cotton. Molly sounds like she's at the other end of a long tunnel when she says, "Are you as stoned as I am?"

The next morning, we feel hung-over and evil. "Morphine tablet next time?" I joke over Wheaties.

Molly rests her head on the table, getting toast crumbs in her hair. "Yeah, good idea."

We stumble through the rest of the day in an exhausted blur, being extra nice to Mom in our shame.

When she was first diagnosed with ovarian cancer two years ago, she sped home and beheaded the flower tops in the garden. When she started her second round of chemotherapy, I took her to Michigan Avenue to shop for expensive wigs made out of real hair. She proclaimed she'd buy the silliest one she could find, blond with two braids. She said she wanted to look like the Swiss Miss Instant Cocoa girl. There was nothing left to do when her doctor told her the cancer had bloomed inside her body. In the car on the drive home from the oncologists', we tried to sing my favorite song from Girl Scout camp, "Heads, shoulders, knees and toes, knees and toes." She leaned her forehead on the passenger window. She said, "What do I do now?" She kept her face away from me, pretending to find the blur of telephone poles interesting. I could think of nothing to say.

I bring home a giant white bakery cake on sale from Jewel Osco with "Happy Bar Mitzvah, Kevin" written in green frosting. I tilt the cake toward Mom. "What do you think, Kevin?" I cut a piece for her. She can't eat it, won't keep it down, but she likes to have it around. I bring the cake close to her nose so she can smell the sugary frosting. Then, I eat the cake for her. She watches the fork travel from the plate to my mouth and back again.

When Mom realized there would be no miraculous recovery at the last second, it was anything goes! An expensive weekend in Cape Cod with lobster for breakfast, red bottles of wine every night of the week (and some lunches). No more library books; we bought hardcover bestsellers. We ordered fabric from New York and a new serger machine for finishing seams. Red meat, juicy hamburgers, Ho Ho's-anything, anything, anything she wanted.

Molly shakes her head at me for buying the cake for Mom; it's not something she would ever do. She thinks she's Mother Teresa because she's been commuting from Kankakee to work for the last ten months. I am the wicked daughter who still bikes to Lake Michigan on the weekends. When we were little, Molly would hoard her Halloween candy and then eat it in front of me after mine was gone, smacking her mouth and saying, "This is so good."

"Your mascara's smeared," I tell her, even though it's not. She reaches up automatically to fix it.

I set the oven timer to ration out her pills. Twenty minutes until her next pain pill. Her hands clench the sheets and she bites her teeth together. She never even used to drink spiked eggnog at Christmas. Now, she looks like a street corner junkie, Come on, man, give it to me. We both watch the too-slow black hand of the living room clock. Fifteen minutes. Ten. I hurry to the kitchen and set the timer off and then run back to help her gulp down the pills with apple juice.

Molly floats into the room cradling the dog in her arms like a baby, even though he is too big and doesn't like it. "It seems a little early for those."

"Molly." She stops. "Who. Gives. A. Fuck."

"Good point," she says. The dog tilts his head back in supplication.

Molly and I sit in the kitchen lighting candles and using the wax to shape long fingernails. We sniff at the sweet burning smell of sulfur left by the matches.

The dog flops on the linoleum. He is tired of all this. No one walks him anymore. He takes advantage of our falling apart and dares to sleep on the living room couch during the day.

Molly opens a cabinet and stands looking in. "What did I want?" The dog stares up too, as bewildered as she is.

"We're losing it," I tell him. His ears perk forward, thinking this might mean we'll give up entirely and feed him raw hamburger. "Bad dog." He thumps his tail. I give him crunchy peanut butter. "Look at his mouth!"

Molly collapses on the kitchen chair, using a fork to trace the outlines of the yellow hen on the placemat Mom made about fifteen kijillion years ago.

Mom begins her nightly keening from the living room. We stay motionless.

"You go," I say.

"You." Molly shoots back. Then, "Should we just kill her?" She bites at the collar of her turtleneck. It's not a real question. There is no life support plug to pull. If we took away the oxygen she occasionally needs, she'd somehow develop gills. The only real way to help her die is for us to stop feeding her or give her an over-dose. Mercy killings happen all the time on movies of the week. There is a lot of weeping, but the viewers know that the daughter/brother/spouse is pumping the loved one full of morphine out of love. The dying patient's eyes shine with gratitude. But, though Molly and I watch those shows like voyeurs at a public hanging and though we admire Doctor Kevorkian, we do not want his phone number.

There are just some things the human body is not built to do.

I put my hand on the crown of Molly's head. "I like your hair cut."

"Thank you." When she leans back against the chair, I miss her, Molly, even though she's right in front of me.

Mom's having trouble speaking. Her breath whistles and she waves her hand in slow circles in the air. We try to guess what she wants. "How many syllables?" Her hands weave with slow motion elegance, like an astronaut waving from the moon. "Is she requesting a hula hoop?" We are getting hysterical, like we did when we were little and used to crank call our neighbors and speak in British accents.

"Keys," she wheezes.

I try to distract her by switching the Virgin Mary night-light off and on. "Mom, look at this." She rocks and howls with her mouth wide open. I feel like putting my hands to my head and joining her, two figures in an Edvard Munch painting. "You want your car keys, Mom? You shouldn't be driving in your condition, but okay."

Even though her keys are on the kitchen counter where I've left them, I search in her purse, an ugly vinyl bag in the hall closet next to her winter coat. Inside: a miniature perfume sample from Chanel, her maroon checkbook, a balled-up Kleenex, a church program from St. Anne's with a perfect lipstick "oh" neatly in the middle, two pennies. In her wallet: ten dollars, a book of stamps with flowers on them, and a picture of Molly, age seven, and me, age ten, at the beach near Lake Michigan. Molly smiles like a girl in a Coppertone ad; my face is screwed up into a scowl. Also, a list of things to do written in her neat block penmanship: buy light bulbs, clothes to Goodwill, contact real estate broker and funeral director, purchase coffin (preferably the iron one), send thank-you notes to Hospice people, fill out insurance forms, call the lawyer. She has thought of everything so we will know how to get it right, like directions on a sewing pattern: pins go this way, cut on the bias against the inside seam, match the dotted lines. No list for what to do when she's gone.

I make Molly go outside with me. We step on the back porch, a blast of cool air hitting our faces. I try to light a cigarette, but can't make the flame catch. Molly grabs the lighter from me, saying, "Here." The blue flame flares bright against her face. For an instant, she is my mother: same round features, wide eyes, and pale English complexion. "What?" she says.

I exhale a white stream of smoke. "What if we throw a funeral and no body shows up? Get it? No body?"

She shrugs and shivers, finally tired of our jokes.

I put on a T-shirt and running shorts and step onto our front lawn. The night air has a weird stillness, like a nuclear explosion has gone off. I consider hot-wiring Molly's Jeep and racing it back to Chicago, the radio turned to "fuck you" heavy metal, my head out the window, following the highway until the tank is empty.

I start to run. My sneakers make heavy thumps on the sidewalk. Past Mrs. Banders' house, past the community center pool, Kankakee high school, big game tonight against Hudson, "Go Falcons," the Woolworth's where I used to shoplift Bonnie Bell lipstick and Vantage cigarettes so Jen Bauer and I could sit under the cover of a weeping willow arguing the merits of staying virgins until our sophomore year. Past the Fred Astaire Dance Studio. The Pizza Hut where I had my first job. I worked there to buy my own clothes so I could escape the jumpers Mom sewed for me or the skirts with calico kitty cats cart-wheeling across the pleats. When vests were in, she made one for me out of butterscotch suede, but then she added colored beads to the ends of the fringe. The beads clacked together when I walked, making me sound like a one-woman maraca show. She never sewed the correct thing; it was always slightly off. She has never gotten it right.

When you're running, the air pushes against your ears and your heart thumps in your chest. If you force yourself past the sweat and the trembling in your legs, you reach a place beyond exhaustion to smooth numbness, where the only thing you think is keep going, keep going, make it to the bushy pine on the corner, past the tree, to the next stop sign and on and on until it feels like you're three feet above the air or orbiting planet Mars.

I pass the unlit window of the fabric store where Mom used to buy Butterick sewing patterns to sew Molly and me matching holiday outfits. I want to throw a rock and shatter the store window, tear down the stenciled sign, erase every trace of these things that remind me of her.

Our closest neighbor, Dr. Max, is an ear, nose and throat specialist at Northwestern though he belongs between the pages of a Lands'

End catalogue. His rugged American face and rower's body make him seem like he might throw a Frisbee at me or drape one of his heavy Shetland wool sweaters around my shoulders. I love him because he sometimes washes his car in his bathrobe and once, when I asked him if we could score some heroin for Mom, he actually thought about it for a minute.

I lean over to catch my breath. A drop of sweat slides from my temple, leaving a salty taste on my lip. Maybe Dr. Max will let me climb on top of him in the yellow grass behind our house. We would do it with medical efficiency and afterward, I could beg him to explain the human body to me, and not just the nose and throat. "What's the hip bone connected to again?" I would ask, and he would show me.

Dr. Max answers his door looking like he's just woken up from a hundred-year nap. I hand him an arrangement of dying white orchids that Molly threw in the trash by our curb. He reads the card. "Thinking of you in your time of need. Signed, the Ladies Book Club." He looks up and holds my gaze. "Thanks."

We sit on the front step. He does not ask how Mom is doing or offer moronic mixed-up condolences such as, Whenever God opens a door, He closes a window.

I tell him I've practiced all of Elizabeth Kubler Ross' stages of death—disbelief, depression, anger, bargaining, acceptance. Molly and I have both been through them so many times that we can diagnose each other in a second. Molly will mope around with unwashed hair and the same cruddy sweatshirt for three days and I'll paddle after her going, "Stage 2. You're at Stage 2 Molly. This is your sister, calling you from Stage 5, Stage 5. Do you read me, Depression?" Molly and I could compete for anything—I bet we could even compete over who recovers from Mom's death faster. Or slower, for that matter.

Dr. Max scratches the raspy unshaved shadow under his chin. I sit on my hands to keep from bolting forward and tracing his clavicle bone with my tongue. "Why do you keep coming back to Kankakee?"

The cold from his cement steps stings the back of my knees. "Because I have to." I know it's true after I say it, though it's not something I've ever voiced out loud.

He says, "Doesn't that piss you off?"

I press the heels of my hands against my eyes until white flashes of light appear. "Yes." I don't have to explain what I really wish for, because we both know the answer already.

When Molly and I were little, we would wrap up anything we could find in old newspaper. Then we would present these objects to Mom as she sat smoking and reading a paperback book at the kitchen table. She'd undo the tape around my gift and put a hand to her heart. "I've been needing a pair of tweezers!" With Molly's, she'd be just as amazed and pleased. "Lava soap! My favorite!"

"But which one do you like *better*?" We'd beg. "If you *had* to pick one, which would you choose?"

She'd answer, "I like them both exactly the same."

"But if you had to pick or you'd be shot to death?"

She'd shake her head and smooth the creases in the newspaper with her hands. "Well, adios then, because I cannot choose."

When I come home, soft Spanish voices transmit from the living room, sounding like a radio broadcast from overseas. The TV is on, giving the room an alien blue glow. The changing images flicker against the wall, dark then light, then dark again. A man's deep tone rumbles from the TV set. I can't understand what he's saying, though it seems if I listen hard enough, I will figure out the words.

Molly is collapsed on the sofa, the dog lying at her feet. She squints at me. She inherited Mom's eyelashes; I have Mom's freckles. The dog exhales in a long, exhausted sigh. "I let him out," Molly says, closing her eyes. I pull the blue star quilt over her shoulders and bend toward her until my nose almost touches her flushed cheek.

During Mom's second round of chemotherapy, before we knew how bad the illness would be, I promised to spend the weekend at home doing our favorite things—going out to people watch and drink bitter coffee at Denny's, renting Charlie Chan movies, making popcorn on the stove and reading books.

I didn't want to go to Kankakee. I wanted to stay home and plot my farewell speech to a man I was sleeping with. We were both unhappy, but unable to separate. A warm body at night seemed preferable to an empty bed.

I stalled until late Saturday and arrived in Kankakee just before the stroke of midnight. I hoped Mom would be asleep and I could have a glass of wine, smoke a cigarette, and collapse in my old room with the collages of thin sun-beam happy girls from *Seventeen* magazine still stuck to the wall.

She was awake, tilted back in the living room recliner with a book on her lap. When I came in, she sat up, straightening her sweatshirt. "Hi, prodigal daughter."

She had lost a lot of hair. Molly told me Mom wouldn't drive in the car with the window down in case it made more hair fall out.

That night, her hair looked odd, standing up from her head like she'd just had an awful scare. I told her I was tired. She said, "That's okay."

When I went to say good-night to Molly in the kitchen, she wouldn't look at me. "What?"

She threw a spoon in the sink, her back to me. "Oh, nothing."

I stayed until about ten the next morning and then left after pancakes Mom made but couldn't eat.

When I turned on the highway back toward the Chicago skyline, a deep sense of relief blossomed in my chest.

Molly called me later that night, after Mom had gone up to bed. I apologized for leaving so early and then made some stupid joke. Molly didn't laugh. She said, "I just think you should know that before you breezed home for your visit, I spent about two hours fixing Mom's hair." She paused to let this sink in. "She's lost most of it but she didn't want you to know. She didn't want to scare you."

Mom's eyes are closed. I wait to see the sheet rise and fall.

There are questions I want to ask her, but I don't want to risk playing out a death bed scene from a black and white B-movie. How do you sew on a zipper? You think you would ask the important questions at some point. How can I tell if I'm in love with someone or just lonely? How did you feel when you met Dad? What were you like when you were little? What will you miss most?

On the Spanish soap opera, Eduardo, wild-eyed, chases after a woman with beautiful black hair flying behind her like a cape. He grabs her arm, "Mi carina." He shakes her. Her head wobbles. "Te quiero," the man says. The woman's mouth stays closed. "Te quiero."

I shut the TV off. She's still asleep. The wristwatch is a faint pulse in the silence. I don't know if it's a gift from my father when he was alive, a family heirloom, or something she bought at a garage sale for ten dollars.

I take her hand. It is cold and light, like a sewing pattern piece. I press the watch to my ear. Hush, the ticking says. Be still.

What She Should Do

*E*veryone in her family assumes Jane's a lesbian, even though she frequently wears skirts and keeps her hair long and her dating history is one long sit-com situation after another. Each holiday dinner, she waits for the pause in conversation before the question is asked by her aunt/grandma/ married cousin(s). "So. . . . Are you seeing anyone right now?"

Jane responds in the way she's rehearsed. "Yes, I see men every day. I see lots of men!" On trains, through the windows of her apartment, in delis, at Penny's Noodle Shop, the 7–Eleven, sitting quietly in flannel shirts in Barnes and Noble reading Pynchon in paperback. They wear black knit caps and have skinny, sensitive wrists. They're also in Borders, The Last Drop Cafe, Ragstock. She wants to run up to them and exclaim, "I'm here all the time! We have so much in common!"

Whoever has asked her the question follows up with: "I just know you're going to find someone amazing one day. Someone who really loves and appreciates you for you!" (When you quit being so needy, desperate, so obviously alone, so willing to accept anything that comes your way. Men have a sixth sense about your lack of expectations, willingness to make coffee in the morning, to offer like a nurse to flush the used condom down the toilet, the way you begin to dress to fit his personality: turtlenecks for the stock market consultant, T-shirts with team logos for the sports fanatic, short plaid skirts held together by safety pins for the aspiring musician.)

Every issue of *Cosmopolitan* offers numerous ways for trapping and keeping a man:

> Be yourself! Men like women who are able to see the humor in all situations and who don't always agree with everything they say. Josh, age 22, explains, "I love it when a girl throws her head back and laughs out loud without caring who hears her. That is so sexy. The biggest turn-on, though, is a girl who knows what she wants and goes after it!"

In real life, this advice does not work. When Jane acts like herself, she is too *something*, too smart or too air-heady, too serious or too jokey, too needy or too distant. She's so busy trying to appear like herself that she becomes someone else.

Her friend, Dustin, who wears Buddy Holly-type glasses, tells her that not all men are like that. She's tried and tried to fall for Dustin, but he's a big soft marshmallow. He would want to cuddle all the time and make her cinnamon toast cut into triangles on Sunday mornings. That would make her want to pinch him and not in a nice way.

What she should do: Give blood every six weeks and wear the "Hug Me, I Gave Blood" heart on her shirt. Find a meaningful job (if she joins the Peace Corps, she might meet "Jake," an earthy man with a scruffy blond beard. They would spend their days educating South Americans about how to grow wheat and their nights in a tent, rubbing mosquito repellent on each other). She should chew gum in public and blow huge pink bubbles. Find an interesting hobby involving beads. Design a poster for a rally at Grant Park. Write free-lance articles concerning the homeless. Develop a dependency problem. Make something creative out of plastic doll heads. Attend poetry readings. Wear Raggedy Ann black and white garter belt stockings. Either quit applying make-up altogether or buy glittery pink false eyelashes. Pick a hockey team and memorize the stats. Purchase a cappuccino maker, a blender for fruit slurpees, a salt-water aquarium, a Black & Decker power drill. Move to Wicker Park. Read Civil War history books. Apply blue nail polish. Learn how to have an orgasm during sex. Have sex. Burn cinnamon-scented candles. Memorize Shakespeare quotes. Stop apologizing when people bump into her.

Wear a monocle, turn into a performance artist, don a cape and a feathered boa, stroll through the city with a gray pet rat on her shoulder, run barefoot in the snow pulling a wooden duck behind her, carry a picket sign on Michigan Avenue with John 3:16 written on it in green marker, smoke a pipe, shave her head, set herself on fire on a subway platform to protest fur coats.

Become a mime who makes balloon poodles on Michigan Avenue or rides a unicycle. Smoke a cherrywood pipe or a hookah. Keep her hair pinned up with sharpened number two pencils and make bracelets out of paper clips.

Walk her cat on leash. Beg for small vials of Coco Chanel from the brittle-masked, smock-wearing woman behind the counter of Marshall Fields. Write a personal ad for the Thursday *Reader*: "Looking for a single, attractive, thirty-something, fiction reading, non-substance abuser artist with fulfilling and well-paying career.

Must be a straight feminist man with a witty sense of humor, a better than average-sized penis, and a well-trained golden retriever. Must also be open to getting married (to me) and providing me wonderful children who you will in no way fuck up with your own issues. No freaks need apply."

Practice laughing with sincerity, learn to read Tarot cards, watch Pink Floyd's *The Wall, Bad Lieutenant,* and *Apocalypse Now* in case anyone should ask her opinion. Read *Starving for Attention* for tips on how to cultivate an eating disorder. Play a tambourine with the Hare Krishnas at O'Hare Airport. Drive a cab. Sign up for a night class in astronomy. Volunteer for Hospice. Take up a cause. Develop a plan. Shoot up. Catch a fatal disease. Swallow heavy prescription drugs. Get a partial lobotomy. Emulate Virginia Woolfe, Anne Sexton, Sylvia Plath.

Anything, anything, anything would be better than what she does right now.

Wanted

*L*ate in the summer, a series of gruesome murders hits Chicago. First, it is one woman's body found. Then two. Then three—triplets named Annabelle, Amber, and Karen. Women are buying Rottweilers and Pit Bulls. They are purchasing stun guns, pepper spray, brass knuckles, screamers, and Chinese stars. Some are even said to carry handguns in their backpacks or rolled up in the sleeves of their raincoats.

Eleanor reads about it first in the subway on her way to work: "Mad Killer on the Loose!" An older lady clutching a canvas bag stuffed with gigantic balls of yarn looks over her shoulder. She makes a "tsk" sound. "What sort of man would do that kind of thing?" Even though it's not officially been stated, everyone has already assumed the killer is male. Eleanor glances at the men nearby, all decent-looking city dwellers with sensible briefcases and colorful ties. The murderer could be any one of them; the man swaying nearby with the cat hair on his jacket, the bearded guy whose wedding ring blinks at her across the aisle, or the boy in the seat in front of her with a chocolate-colored mole on his neck. The thought gives her a tickling little thrill along the base of her spine.

It is not easy being single in Chicago—couples walk languidly down the bike path on Lake Michigan, hold hands across the small round tables at Starbucks, argue passionately in heated whispers between train stops on the El, and make up with wet kisses. Eleanor is twenty-nine and can see the rest of her future unspooling before her—how she will start to glower at young couples, refuse the wedding invitations of her high school friends, start drinking by herself and weeping over home mortgage commercials, how her ovaries will shrivel up into tiny little walnuts, unused, unneeded.

It's not as if she doesn't have opportunities. She meets men all the time in her job at the psychological intake center. The problem with those men is that they are all psychotic and medicated at varying levels of stability. Sweet, for the most part, except when they go off their meds and call the office demanding someone to come over and get Jesus off their living room sofa or threaten to stick needles in their eyeballs to stop the sound of Muzak stuck in their heads. She develops sympathetic crushes on them, nothing serious, but enough to make her feel like she is still capable of love and will not under any circumstances become her Aunt Ann who, at age 51, has taken to dating every man on the planet she meets on Match.com, loving them for two months, and then getting her heart broken into a million worn-out pieces. She embarks on a two-month gin binge, sobering up only after losing her entire paycheck at the slot machines. Poor Aunt Ann! Poor

Eleanor who may have somehow gotten Ann's genetic inability to meet someone nice who is not married, gay, or a psychotic freak.

Here's who she has dated over the last two years since moving to Chicago to escape her too-clingy, too sweet, too married boyfriend in Florida: An Armenian dental student who said, "It's not that I don't want to be with anyone. It's just that I don't want to be with *you*." The method actor who told her she resembled a young Elizabeth Taylor, adding that she probably needed to watch her weight as well. Two blind dates set up by friends, both named Todd and both flamingly gay. The punk rocker who slapped her ass while they were making out and gave her six raspberry-sized hickies on her collarbone like a necklace. The red-headed chubby guy who burst into tears over his ex-wife at a restaurant. (Did she go out with any of these men again? Yes, in fact, she did.)

Her friend Renee tells her she needs to be more discriminating. "It's like you get the information early on that the guy is a freak, and then you continue to date him anyway."

"But they seem kind of nice at first."

"I'm sure Eva Braun said the same thing about Hitler. 'Oh, he's super sweet once you get to know him. He makes a great omelet!'"

Then she meets Adam in the grocery store just like the articles in women's magazines say you can—right by the meat section in Jewel Osco. They reach for a package of raw hamburger at the same time, their fingers nearly touching. "Oh, sorry," they say together. She sizes him up. He has a scruffy cinnamon-colored goatee, and wears worn Levis and a white T-shirt that says "Stop Reading My T-shirt." It could be him. Her future groom. Or it could be him, the serial killer. Eleanor has to pinch her thigh to keep from bursting into a fifty-watt smile at the sudden possibilities.

Emboldened by the outside chance she could be this close to death, she tells him she's surprised to meet someone nowadays who's not a vegetarian.

"No, I eat raw meat right out of the package." He smiles, his teeth sharp and beautiful white. He hands her the hamburger. His knuckles have a splattering of sweet pinpoint freckles across them. "You buy the meat. I'll pay for the hamburger buns."

"Thanks." She stares into his eyes, which are slanted and dark blue like the ocean.

He walks her home. He tells her he's a first-year medical resident at Northwestern University currently in his surgical rotation which, he explains, mostly consists of learning how to slice people open. He has seen the inside of the human body, a beating heart, the large purple slab of a kidney, the fragile inroads of capillaries and blood vessels. Much better than the last guy she dated who lived at home while writing his autobiography and working as a waiter at TGIFridays and who always smelled like French fries. Their future unfolds for her as they weave their way past the sprinkling of homeless people and tattooed teens loitering on the street corners. She will be a good doctor's wife, thoughtful and giving, and never complaining when she has to wash his blood-stained shirts by hand.

He doesn't try to hold her hand, but when she steps out onto the curb, nearly colliding with a bicyclist in serious Spandex who has whizzed around the corner, he pulls her back, saving her from certain disfigurement or at the very least the embarrassment of being run over by a ten-speed. "Now I've saved your life. You owe me yours."

At her apartment door, he shakes her hand. An electric shock jolts up her spine. When was the last time she's been touched? She remembers the week before in the same grocery store, letting out a puppyish yelp as someone's coat sleeve brushed her arm in the express line. "I'd like to see you again," he says. He has a vulnerable, heart-shaped face and a slight overbite that she wants to run her tongue over.

"Okay," she writes her phone number on his wrist with her black-tipped pen. "Never wash this away," she commands.

"I won't," he answers. She scurries into her building, a squeal of glee in her throat as if he were chasing her.

And later, right before she goes to bed, when she glances out the window and sees a figure out by the darkened lamppost (might be him, it's really too dark to see), she tells herself it wouldn't be bad if he's still there. She decides it's interesting instead. She pulls the shade down and considers her little life, the too many cat toys scattered like bodies across the floor, the stacks of overdue library books, the half-finished mugs of chamomile tea on her coffee table. "He may be a serial killer, but he's *my* serial killer," she tells the cat. The cat responds with a noncommittal meow—might be agreement or might be a warning—it's hard to say for sure.

The first time they have sex, he asks if he can wear leather gloves.

"What?" She has purchased special underwear for the occasion, slightly naughty black lace with a kitty cat face on the front.

"Unless that makes you uncomfortable." He hovers above her, his arms trembling. A dark blue vein pulses in his pale neck.

She grasps his arms to stop the shaking. "I don't mind the gloves."

He places his index finger along the soft hollow behind her ear. The pointed tip of the leather glove may leave faint scratches along her body like hieroglyphics. "This is your circulation system," he says. A shiver of goose bumps breaks across her skin. That's a rabbit running across your grave, her mom used to say. He presses lightly beneath her jaw. "Here is your carotid artery." She can feel the thrum of her heart against his fingertips. "Your heart, you know, is the size of your fist." He moves his finger across the hill of her throat, along her esophagus to the dip in her collarbone. He shows her exactly how the aorta of the heart circulates blood to the rest of the body—each chamber pumping blood in and out, to be sure it reaches every part of the body down to the tips of the fingers and toes.

"Why can't we meet him?" her friend Renee (still single, still looking) asks during a smoke break at work. "Does he have a club foot? Is he hunch-backed and dwarfish? What exactly do you see in him?"

"He's . . ." What is it exactly? His eyes are blue. She has always liked blue eyes. His hair curls along the collar of his shirt. He can imitate all kinds of accents—regional ones even. He stops to pet every dog they pass in the street. He told her he used to think a roach clip was an elaborate way to trap and release bugs. He has been to the opera and the theatre and liked both; he wears argyle socks ironically, enjoys black-and-white movies starring Cary Grant. Didn't rush to fuck her. Doesn't own a money clip or silly cartoon ties or wear reflective motorcycle sunglasses. Can do the *New York Times* Sunday crossword in pen. Chops carrots well. Thinks sharks have gotten a bad rap. Knows things about the human body that your average person would be amazed by. Has not yet called her a bitch, given her a black eye, or attempted to strangle her with a bit of chicken wire. "He's interesting," she tells Renee. "And he likes me." And that, as far as she can see, is that.

For the first two months, it's slightly wonderful. She can now speak with condescending hopefulness to the single girls at work. When she sees men on the train, she no longer has to wonder if they think she's pretty, if she is reading an interesting enough novel, if she has a workable reproductive system. Now she has dates on Saturday nights and someone to call after she finishes work. So what if sometimes he does strange things like laughing when someone gets shot on a TV show or else crying over a

Michelin tire commercial, his face buried in his hands. "What is it?" she asks.

"Nothing." Just like that, the wailing noises shut off, like someone pulling the plug out while vacuuming.

She calculates the days they've dated, then the weeks, each additional week bringing her closer to—what? Success! Children! A car! A house in the suburbs with central air. A respite from her worried mother calling from a thousand miles away, her voice faint across the wires.

Her mother phones one Sunday night to tell her that they're cleaning out her old bedroom closet. Does Eleanor want her old Barbie dolls sent up? They might be worth something, though half of them have had their heads sheared and different colored marker streaked across their plastic faces. And what about her china doll with the cracked face? She used to love that doll. Her mother remembers when she got it . . .

Eleanor barely listens. She has her attention turned to the TV, where a breaking news story has interrupted the rerun of *Law and Order Special Victims Unit.* Another pretty girl gone missing—last seen by her friends at the Cubby Bear bar in Wrigleyville. They flash the girl's photo. She's a blond skinny girl with a cheerleader smile.

She didn't see Adam last night even though they had plans to go to a matinee of *Sweeney Todd.* He called her at the last minute, using a suspicious-sounding scratchy voice, claiming the flu. Has she seen him on any of the nights of the murders? She must start keeping track. She may need to provide evidence. She may be called to the witness stand one day, where she will sit in a newly purchased black suit, clutching one of her grandmother's embroidered handkerchiefs, and confessing bravely, that yes, yes, yes, it must be him.

Her mother interrupts her thoughts. "Well, what do you think?"

"I think it's a grand idea!" she answers.

Her mother says nothing for a moment. She clears her throat. "Honey, are you okay? Are you happy? Do you need me to send you cat food coupons?"

"Yes, I'm happy!" Eleanor crows in response. She does a little barefoot tap dance on the floor, scaring the cat. "I'm so happy I could just die."

She suggests they stay at his apartment for one night. He sniffles, claiming to still be suffering from the flu and possibly bronchitis now. He has many explanations. It's a basement apartment and prone to mildew. The tub has leaked and seeped into the carpet and it will take several weeks for the landlord to fix it. The dog above him barks all night long. "Anyway, I prefer to stay with you here," he gestures wildly to her living room, the second-hand futon with frayed white and pink quilt, the old crate fashioned as a coffee table, the bookshelves made out of two step ladders. Pictures she's cut out from a childhood copy of *Alice and Wonderland*—the Cheshire Cat, the Queen of Hearts saying, Off with her head! Scotch taped haphazardly to the flaking white walls.

She pictures his apartment chock full of elaborate torture devices, chains dangling from the ceilings, a set of sharpened butcher knives arranged by size on coffee table, and a miniature fridge containing carefully labeled body parts: "Limping Girl's Right Kneecap." Boxes of clothing and accessories would be stacked along the walls. Everyone knows serial killers like mementos— bright red fingernails, women's used pantyhose, black pumps with worn down heels. The last accent pieces of the dead. Or maybe she would find nothing that reveals who he is or why she likes him, if she even really does. Her heart is a closed fist, a mysterious thing even to her. It doesn't seem to feel things the way a heart should.

The killings grow more gruesome. Now they are finding just parts of women's bodies. A girl's head discovered half buried along the gritty shoreline of Lake Michigan. Another girl's arm, the wrist with an Anne Klein Roman numeral watch still ticking, found sticking out of a garbage can on Halsted Street. The bottom half of a young woman's jaw, still covered in Violent Sunset lipstick. She had a good orthodontist; her teeth are perfectly straight. No cavities. She was engaged to be married in just one month. A real tragedy.

The *Tribune* dubs him the Bits and Pieces Killer. A psychologist on CNN describes the typical profile of a serial murderer: he's most likely a white male between the ages of 19 and 45 who maintains an outward profile of normalcy but who may have a history of abuse or neglect. He can function well in society, though he may also have moments of paranoia or extreme emotional mood swings. "He can hold down a job," explains the expert whose thick eyebrows sprawl like a fuzzy caterpillar across his forehead. "Friends and close relatives are often surprised to learn that the person they've thought they've known for years has been systematically dismembering in his basement instead of building cabinets." Adam fits some of the criteria. Come to think of it though, pretty much every guy she has dated could match this profile.

She stares at her pale face in the bathroom mirror, practicing various expressions—disdain, anger, fear, widening her eyes, coating her mouth with dark red lipstick and shaping her mouth into an "oh" for "noooooooooo." She puckers her lips. If he is the killer, why doesn't he want to kill her? What's wrong with *her*? Is she not pretty enough to kill?

While he's in the shower singing a complicated song from an opera, she rummages through his backpack. She finds a pair of unisex eyeglasses, a medical textbook about surgical technique, gauze, an unopened jumbo box of Trojan condoms ribbed for her pleasure, and finally, in a black case, she discovers a scalpel, clean and sharp. Are they allowed to check scalpels out of the hospital like some kind of library privileges for med students? She takes the scalpel out of the case, admiring the way the blade glimmers in the slanting afternoon light. She puts it away and begins rummaging through the front pocket of the pack.

"What are you doing?" She jumps. He stands in her hallway, a white towel wrapped around his waist, wet drops splashing on the floor.

"Getting to know you! Getting to know all about you!" She belts out.

He looks back at her with blank blue eyes. Now he will do it. She looks around for an object of defense. Nothing. Nothing. Her apartment is stocked with only spongy things, throw pillows and half unraveled balls of yarn. It is the apartment of someone too soft—too full of cat paraphernalia and bookshelves filled with paperbacks by Stephen King alongside soft-core romantic pornography where the sex is so muted that you can't tell if the characters are fucking or just wrestling enthusiastically.

Her shoulders tense. She hasn't made an escape plan should he leap at her throat. If she's quick enough, she can grab the nearby thrift store lamp and smack him over the head. Or just show the ugly lamp to him, hold it up to him like Van Helsing with a crucifix, offend his aesthetic sensibilities. A hiccup of laughter escapes her mouth.

Adam moves towards her, but instead of grabbing her, he picks up his backpack, zippers it closed, and says, his lips barely moving. "You don't have to be so weird about everything. If you want to know something about me, try asking."

But that's the problem. She's not sure she wants to know.

Later that week, he tells her he wants to tie her up to a ladder-back chair. She should wear only her bra and underwear. He would also like it if she would put on a silk blindfold. He turns off all the lights and wraps a silk scarf around her eyes. He ties her arms loosely behind her back with red Christmas ribbon. It's a chilly summer night and so he allows her to leave on her socks. He leans over and whispers in her ear, "Do you know the adult human body has 206 bones give or take a few? The clavicle, the sternum, twenty-four vertebrae, twelve ribs . . ." His voice presses hot and tickling on the back of her neck.

"And which bone would you say is your favorite?" she jokes.

"Don't move until I tell you." The tip of his tongue touches her ear. She shudders with pleasure and revulsion.

Something changes in the air. He's moved away from her. She listens to the soft hissing of the radiator and the muted whoosh of cars passing in the street below. The neighbor above is playing music, something slow and mesmerizing. Her arms start to tremble. Something thuds on the floor in the next room. Her heart paddles in her chest. She anticipates the cool tip of a scalpel at her throat. Behind her closed eyelids, white dots of light sputter. Another faint noise from the bedroom. Is he searching for a weapon? She strains against the ribbons. They slip away easily. She folds her hands in her lap. She waits for a long time, until she starts to shiver.

She unwraps the scarf, her head pounding slightly. She waits for her vision to adjust to the new dark of the living room expecting to see him crouched and waiting to pounce. The cat's yellow eyes glow back at her from the hump of the living room sofa. Other than that, the room is empty.

He's stretched out on her bed fully dressed except for his sneakers. He's reading her college copy of *Heart of Darkness*. She throws the scarf at him, but she's too far away and they both watch as the scarf falls to the floor in a slippery heap. "It was an experiment," he explains. "I wanted to see how long you'd wait."

This is the moment where she should break up with him. This should be the last straw. And if it were happening to someone else, if it were a play she were reading or a story her friend told, she would scream if the girl didn't throw him out or kick him in the head. But since it's just her life, and no one (really) is watching, she picks up the scarf, folds it, and places it back in her dresser.

A special news report interrupts the Thursday night whodunit on TNT. It appears the killer may have struck again. The male newscaster, a cheese-cakey blond with a gigantic chin, is exhilarated by the news, almost breathless. This time, the killer has left a cardboard box on the back stairs of a gray stone monastery on Belmont Avenue. Nestled inside the box and wrapped in red tissue paper is a human heart. Doctors have not yet determined the gender of the heart, but chances are good that it belongs to a woman.

Eleanor turns off the TV. Why are the hearts sent on Valentines Day so unlike the real ones? Real hearts are red and purple, veined and misshapen, like rutabagas. A heart is not a beautiful thing, at least not until you get inside and see how complicated it is and how much work it must do to keep one body alive.

Though she hasn't been there herself, she knows where he lives.

She walks the twelve blocks to his apartment and presses the buzzer. He answers immediately, as if he were standing just inside the door waiting for her arrival. He has shaved off his goatee, leaving his face bare. He looks much younger. Without a word, he stands aside to let her in.

It's a studio apartment with three small curtain-less windows that face an alleyway. He has a tiny kitchen with a miniature oven, dingy refrigerator, and a card table with two folding chairs. There's a small white door on the far wall, which may be a closet or the bathroom. No furniture except for a futon mattress on the floor with a tangle of sheets at the bottom and three or four stacks of books towering knee high. No severed heads used as hat racks, no little children locked up in rabbit hutches, no mobiles made out of body parts, not one sharp implement in sight. "Oh," Eleanor says after she's had a look around. The room has an unpleasant odor, part mildew, part sour milk, and part sweaty socks.

He sits on one of the folding chairs. "I guess you understand now why I don't host more dinner parties." The blasé way he's leaning back on the chair feels fake, like he's pretending to be comfortable. Despite the fact that she's in his apartment, she feels like she could rummage through his cupboards and stuff her face with his Ritz crackers.

If he just says one nice or slightly interesting thing, she'll stay. They wait together. The faucet from the sink drips.

He scratches under his chin. It appears he has forgotten he's shaved off his beard and now has an entirely new face. He says, "Would you ever let me pee on you?"

She sees it—he's an every day, nasty, Jack-in-the-Box surprise of a human being. He doesn't even fit the basic criteria of a nice, quiet guy with homicidal tendencies.

On one of his windowsills sits a sad little plant with wrinkled brown leaves, the only thing he may have succeeded in killing. She walks over to it and sees that it hasn't been watered in days and days. The soil is dry and crumbles between her fingers. Still, a few of the stems are strong and green. She turns back to him. He hasn't moved. "I guess I'm going now." He says nothing. "Best of luck to you in the future." They blink at each other for a second.

When she leaves, she carries the plant with her, daring him to tell her no.

She steps out of the building, carefully avoiding a pile of trash someone has dumped near the curb. For a brief second, she imagines him pursuing her, his hot hands grabbing her throat and dragging her into the bushes. In her heart of hearts, she knows he won't follow her. For this, she discovers she is relieved.

A full moon lights up the city, which remains busy despite how late it is. Pigeons, living bowling pins with feet, peck at a nearby scattering of breadcrumbs. A man on the corner waves for a cab. On the other side of the street, the Clark bus leaves the curb with a Godzilla-like roar, the faces of the people blurring as it hurries away. In the distance, Eleanor can just see the pinnacle of the Sears Tower and the surrounding skyscrapers whose lit windows will stay on long after everyone has fallen asleep. She walks towards it and towards home.

She puts her hand over her heart as he taught her. It beats.

In Mem

$\mathcal{M}$em's name is short for Memory, which Mrs. Pototnick, her third grade teacher at the new school, calls "ironic" because Mem has a hard time remembering anything—the names of all the major internal organs, where Illinois appears on the United States map, the street address of her aunt's house where she's living now. These are important things. They are on tests and are part of fitting into the real world. Mrs. Pototnick cracks down hard on the facts. They learn how to use grammar, which presidents did what, and ways to measure distance in inches, feet, and miles. Also: what's the quickest animal? The cheetah, but don't ask what the cheetah is running from or to, if the cheetah chases girls, if there are any tactics to avoid cheetahs, like say, tucking yourself into a small ball as they advise for grizzly bears. If she ran a school, Mem would gear it only toward real-life survival tips: In the Wilderness, At Home, When You Find a Lump.

Other tips: In a lightning storm, stay away from open fields and don't carry an umbrella. If a tornado approaches, run to the nearest ditch and lie face down. The tornado may pass. You might hear a moment of pure silence in the eye of it. If a ball rolls out onto the street, look both ways and ask yourself, Is the ball more important than your own life? Don't climb a ladder wearing socks. Don't remove an arrow on your own. Find out your allergies as soon as possible. A simple bee sting could be the end of you. Don't act scared about performing mouth-to-mouth on an ugly person. This is life and death we're talking about here, not a beauty contest. By all means, don't spread honey all over your body and lie down on a fire ant hill.

When Mrs. Pototnick first introduced Mem to the class, she said, "And this is Memory who will be staying at school for awhile until her mom gets better." This sounded to Mem like at 3 o'clock when the final bell rang, she would remain at school, waving good-bye to the other children from the classroom window and then spending the night stretched out on a spongy mat in the middle of the gym floor rather than returning to her aunt's.

The kids stared back at her. "My mom's not dead or anything," Mem reassured them. "It's not like in *Bambi*." The class of children looked at her as if she has just landed on Earth after being raised on a planet outside of the solar system. That was when Mem noticed Wendy Fogley, sitting in the front row, not smiling, her hands neatly crossed on the desk like the littlest and fussiest of nuns.

It is hard to believe Marguerite and Mem's mom are sisters. Marguerite writes numbers in marker by the phone because she's always losing slips of paper. The numbers scrawl across the wall in different colors, fancy curlicues on the "5's" and "7's." She wears long billowing pants that make whooshing noises. When Mem's aunt talks to strangers at the Natural Foods Co-op, she crows things like, "I like the thump of a good papaya!" Once, they were in the grocery store and Mem noticed near the frozen food section that Marguerite was wearing a brown shoe on one foot and a black shoe on the other one. When Marguerite's not teaching piano, she plays her own music. Her hands fly from one end of the keyboard to the other so fast, the fingers blur. While she waters her ferns, she sings "I've Got a Brand New Pair of Roller Skates!" at the top of her lungs in a way that is embarrassing to watch. She acts nothing like Mem's mom; even her hair is wrong. She keeps it in a long ponytail, more like a girl than a grown woman. But with her hair pulled up, Marguerite looks a lot like Mem's mother, except not as skinny. When she lets go, her hair tumbles in wavy, knotted strands of brown and white to the middle of her back. Mem once wanted to grow her hair like Rapunzel's, long enough to touch the floor.

Sometimes, Mem hears Marguerite counting out beats with one of her piano students and freezes, because her voice sounds familiar.

Tiny black ants crawl across the kitchen cabinet in a straight line, up to where her aunt stashes whole-wheat cookies, bran, and brown rice. Marguerite leaves toast crumbs for the ants to carry on their backs "They're not hurting anyone, Pumpkin-pie." She twirls on the crooked wooden floor in bare feet. She asks Mem if she wants to lure the ants out onto the porch with blocks of brown sugar cubes.

Mem says, "Thank you, but no thank you." It is important to be polite. It is called manners and it will get you far.

When Marguerite goes upstairs, Mem watches the ants march across the counter like a small, determined army. She squashes as many as she can, whapping them under the sole of her sneaker, thinking with each thump, Dead, dead, dead.

When Mem first arrived, she thought Marguerite was the blue fairy from *Pinocchio*, because she wore a long blue nightgown like the illustration in the book and stayed up with her the first few nights when Mem had bad dreams. But now, when Mem sees her sitting cross-legged in the middle of the floor with her palms turned upward, she can't remember why she ever thought that. The vanilla-scented smoke curls from the tip of the incense stick, reminding her of the caterpillar in *Alice in Wonderland* with his hookah saying, "Who are you?"

Mrs. Pototnick tells them to turn in a story about their favorite person. Mem writes about a girl in a program she and Marguerite watched the night before on PBS. It was about spina bifida and the main person was Sarah, who was eight. She lived with a hole in her back and had to crawl across the floor in diapers. In her report, Mem explains how Sarah is independent for someone like this, but could die at any moment. She draws a picture of Sarah sitting in a wheelchair, holding a single red rose in her hand. Above this, she writes, "Will I ever walk again???"

Mrs. Pototnick collects the papers and shuffles through to choose a few to read out loud in class. She picks stories about the President of the United States, the Best Father in the World, Wonder Woman, Jesus. Mem's story is not one of them.

That night, Mem dreams Sarah is stuck under the bed with her spine oozing jelly on the floor. She tries to convince Sarah it's not as bad as it seems. At least she will never have to take gym. But Sarah doesn't believe her. She keeps crying and crying. "But what will I do? What will I do?"

The only good part of her new life is Wendy Fogley. Wendy Fogley has long blond curls that spring around her shoulders like a girl in an old fashioned book, socks with stars on them, and jeans with butterflies stitched on the back pockets. Some days, Wendy wears a pair of red Mary Jane shoes. She has a pink Barbie lunch box with straps. Her lunches are a dream come true. Peanut butter-filled celery, ham and cheese sandwiches with Miracle Whip on Wonder Bread, and for dessert, Oreos or Ding Dongs.

Mem gives herself tests. If she can button her jacket before Marguerite finishes singing, "O Sole Mio," in the shower, Wendy Fogley will want to be her partner when they line up after lunch. If she plays the C-minor scale without messing up, Wendy will ask to copy her multiplication quiz. Holding her breath for sixty seconds, eating a spoonful of wheat germ without gagging, hanging from the pull-up bar until her arms tremble—all of these tasks, if performed correctly, are signs that Wendy and she will become best friends.

During social studies, Mem asks Wendy if she would like to peel the scab on her knee. If Mem is lucky, it might leave a scar, so even if Wendy Fogley never likes her, Mem will have the mark on her leg to remember her by forever.

Wendy wrinkles her nose, which is sprinkled with cinnamon-colored freckles. "Where are you from?" She turns back to face the front of the class, her arm shooting in the air to answer a question about the Pilgrims.

Mem ducks down, pretending to look for something, and picks at the corner of the scab with her fingernail, pulling, pulling. A piece peels away from her skin. She holds her breath and rips the whole thing off at once. The white space fills with blood. Mem lets the blood trickle down her leg in one thin line, feeling sick and triumphant.

The next day, Wendy Fogley hands out birthday invitations. Every girl in the class receives one, even wheezy Melissa with the heart murmur and lazy eye. The card shows a sleek, long-eyelashed Siamese cat with a big red bow and slanted blue eyes. The cat says, "It's a *purrfect* time for a party." Inside is the date of the party and Wendy Fogley's address written in straight, grown-up penmanship.

At the party, Wendy Fogley and Mem will hold hands and sit next to each other. Or maybe Wendy will be allowed to ask one girl and one girl only to spend the night and that person will be Mem. They could stay up until Wendy's parents have gone to bed and sneak out at the stroke of midnight and go to the playground, or ride bikes to the municipal pool and see a shooting star on the way back and make a wish and Wendy Fogley would like Mem so much that she would let her move in or stay out back in a shed.

At recess, after everyone else has gone outside to throw balls at one another, Mem sneaks into the coat closet. She puts her nose against Wendy Fogley's red raincoat, inhaling its sweet, plastic smell.

Mem waits for news of her mother. She can't stop thinking of her as "mother," even though she always called her "mom" in real life. It's like she's a character in book about orphans. None of it feels real at all.

The night before the party, she dreams that it is a surprise for her. The students all line up to tell her how much they like her. "I love your tennis shoes!" says Jennifer B. with the lisp. "You always have the greatest lunches," another tells her. The line of kids goes on and on. Each time someone says something nice, it's like a tiny, star-shaped cookie cutter imprints itself on her heart. Thank you! The last girl is Wendy Fogley. She refuses to shake Mem's hand. She stands with her hand on her hip and speaks in the same voice that carries across the playground at recess, telling everyone where to stand during Four Square. "You know this is just a dream, right? None of this will ever come true in real life. Not even once before you die." Wendy Fogley smiles, showing the black gap in her mouth where her baby tooth has fallen out.

Mem wakes up with the sheets tangled in her legs. It takes her a minute to remember where she is. Then she hears the low, faint whistle of her aunt's snores on the other side of the thin bedroom wall. Sometimes, Mem can fall back asleep if she forces herself to remember every detail of the old apartment, starting with the front door and moving through each square inch of the rooms. The pantry door that won't shut, the kitchen with the blue cabinets, the alphabet magnets on the fridge, her mother's library books in a row next to her bed. But she can't quite picture the tile in the bathroom (does it have green or blue squares?) or how photos are arranged on the bookshelves in the living room. She must go through each detail again and again to fix them in her brain before they escape her forever.

The day of the party finally arrives. Mem wears her best outfit. It's white with a sailor collar and a red tie that hangs down the front. If only she had black tap shoes. That would be even better; that would be heaven. Marguerite braids her hair, exclaiming, "Voila!" when she finishes, and holding up a hand mirror so Mem can view the two neat rows down her back. "You are an extraordinary child," Marguerite tells her. "I may have to keep you." She squeezes her hard. Mem takes in her pine cone and cherry cough drop smell before slipping away.

Marguerite follows her into the living room. "I got you some Wendy Fogley presents for the party," she trills, tick-tocking a yellow plastic bag from Walgreens. She pulls each item out with a "Ta-da!" She lines the presents on the coffee table. "Jacks. Paddle ball. Barbie in bathing suit. Puzzle book with 300 pieces.

And a kazoo." Mem feels sick. She pictures Wendy Fogley's sneer as she unwraps each gift. "You girls could play with some of these things if the party gets boring."

"Oh, okay. Thank you." That is the polite thing to say. She puts all the gifts back in the bag. She goes into the bedroom and shoves the bag as far back into the closet as it will go, underneath the long coats and shoeboxes and wrinkled wrapping paper.

In the farthest corner of the closet, she has stashed some things from home—two hand-written notes from her mom that she found in her lunch box, a miniature porcelain doll with a white bonnet, a fuzzy rabbit bank with bald patches that's filled with fifty-cent pieces. The gold necklace her mom gave her rests in the center of a green velvety jewelry box. Two tiny hearts swing from the chain. Mem wraps the box in brown grocery bag paper. She covers the paper with horse heads and balloons. She draws excellent horse heads. She adds a stripe on one horse and a short mane on another. The smell of the marker is sharp and clean and good. She licks the end of it and runs to the bathroom mirror to look at the black line down the middle of her tongue like a tattoo.

Mem has Marguerite drop her off at the corner, because the muffler on the VW sounds like a jet plane landing. Marguerite spits on her fingers and smoothes Mem's eyebrows. Mem shrinks against the car door. "Please be careful about the ice cream. Too much might give you a stomach-ache."

"Okay." Mem plans on eating everything, no matter what.

Wendy Fogley lives in a huge white house with columns on the front just like in colonial days. Mrs. Fogley answers the door and tells her to please come in, please, please, and what a pretty dress. Mem loves Mrs. Fogley. She smells strong, like expensive perfume bought from one of the round glass cases in department stores. A superstar Mom—red, red, lipstick, a real-looking gold necklace, two gold bracelets like Cleopatra, flowing clothes that appear slippery to touch.

Everything in their house is like a movie. Carpet on the floors, no speck of dust, and for sure no ants in the kitchen. Mem follows Mrs. Fogley through the house, praying her shoes are not leaving mud tracks across the white carpet.

Downstairs, girls cluster in small groups: Kim, Lisa, three Jennifers, two Julies, an Eileen, a Courtney, a Heather and a few others whose names begin with J's or K's. Melissa, the eye-patch girl, is not there. Mem's stomach sinks. Clearly, she is now the worst one.

Her hands shake and the tips of her fingers feel cold, her palms sweaty. She thrusts the box at Wendy. "You can open it, if you want. It's a necklace." Wendy says thank you. She puts the present on top of a bigger square box with a pink bow the size of a cabbage.

The entire basement is decorated with pink and white streamers, pink and white balloons, pink cardboard plates and matching cups and napkins, and a "Happy Birthday" sign strung together in separate letters from the ceiling. Gifts tower near a table with a Barbie tablecloth, Barbie's big blond, smiling head dotting along the edges.

The girls stand around with their arms dangling at their sides like they're waiting to get picked for softball. No one seems to be having a good time yet except for Courtney who—Mem overheard someone say—peed her pants after missing the word "umbrella" in a spelling bee in second grade. Courtney whose older brother always has detention or suspension and Courtney whose mother is divorced. Courtney who Mem suspects wants to be her friend.

Mrs. Fogley claps her hands. "Okay, girls, let's play a game!"

They are made to participate in several games with Mrs. Fogley explaining the rules for each one. They balance hard-boiled eggs on spoons, two teams racing each other across the blue shag carpet. They twirl around and try to pin-the-tail on the donkey. They play musical chairs.

They can choose from Coca-Cola, Sprite, lemonade, red Hi-C fruit punch, Doritos in plastic bowls and Cheetos. Mem stands by the food table chomping one Cheeto after another until her fingers turn orange. They eat a store-bought cake with white frosting, thick blue flowers, and yellow cursive letters spelling out "Happy Birthday, Wendy!"

The phone rings and Mrs. Fogley disappears upstairs. Wendy leans against the wall. Nobody is saying anything.

"This is a great party!" Mem chirps.

Wendy Fogley says, "Let's say who I like the best from favorite to least favorite." One long sausage curl has grown longer than the others and dangles over her shoulder. What would it be like to take hold of one of the curls and stretch it out from her head as far as possible? "I like Kim best. Then Jennifer B." She surveys the room. "Skinny Julie. Jennifer T. Then Heather . . ." She continues on, pausing every once in a while to tap her fingers against her lips. Her blue eyes land on Mem. "Mem. . . . Then Courtney, and I guess Melissa last, because she's a retard."

They giggle. Mem giggles too though she feels sick.

Wendy's eyes again flicker toward Mem. "Don't you live in that house with all the dandelions?"

"I don't live there." Mem's tongue sticks to the roof of her mouth. "I sleep in a tree house in the back yard."

Wendy Fogley rolls her eyes. "I'm sure."

"I swear." She crosses her heart and hopes to die. She tells them where she really lives is with her mother, and they have nine cats named after all of Santa's reindeer, three purebred bloodhounds, and four white quarter horses. They own a cabin in the forest with apple trees near a blue lake where they swim for hours in the summer. Sometimes, they see a tail flash in the water; it could be a mermaid, maybe not, but it's definitely not a fish. There is a window on the roof of the cabin, and at night, they lie on the wet grass and stare up at the sky searching for the Big Dipper. Then they talk until it's morning again, and eat French toast with strawberries for breakfast and drink real coffee.

"Lie," Wendy pronounces. Her curls have flattened against her head.

"Get me a needle. I'll prick my finger if it's not true."

Wendy takes one of the darts from the game of "Pin-the-Tail-on-the-Donkey" and hands it to Mem. "Go ahead."

The girls gather in a close circle. Mem holds the dart pointing down, like you're supposed to do when running with scissors. She makes sure Wendy Fogley is watching her. She jabs the dart into her palm, hard, quick, pretending it's a tetanus shot. A small blossom of blood rises in the center of her hand like a tiny red flower. A flush of heat ripples from her toes to the top of her head. Mem moves in slow motion, everything dreamy and out of focus, to the corner of the room. She knows what comes next and tries to think of the right thing to do in a situation like this. She starts to pull off her dress and staggers toward the table lined with gifts. She watches it happen from outside herself, feeling sorry for that poor girl getting sick. Out comes the birthday cake, the red Hi C, potato chips and what looks like a little piece of apple. Wendy yells, "Mom!"

Mrs. Fogley appears, "Oh, Christ." She throws a handful of pink Barbie napkins on top of the mess and thumps Mem on the back as though trying to dislodge a piece of hamburger. The row of pale faces watch them as they go up the stairs, all of them a blur except for Wendy who looks at Mem like she wishes she'd drop dead.

She is exiled to Wendy's bedroom. The shades are drawn and the room is blue and quiet. It smells like Love's Baby Soft perfume. She's too sick to even care about the stenciled daisies along the border of the ceiling or the pink and white checked bedspread and canopy or the vanity mirror or the jewelry box.

Mem holds the wet washcloth to her forehead. This must be what it feels like to be in the hospital, everything fuzzy and like you're trapped in a cocoon, so far away that it's hard to remember anything about your real life.

Mrs. Fogley comes in with a fizzing glass of ginger ale. "Would you like to call your aunt?" Mem doesn't know how to tell Mrs. Fogley that she can't remember the phone number. She gives her the old number instead.

"That's long distance, dear."

Mem pretends to fall asleep. Mrs. Fogley dials a number from Wendy's white princess phone and whispers. "You'll have to take her. I don't think she knows her own phone number." Mem squints. Mrs. Fogley sighs and looks at herself in Wendy's heart-shaped mirror, pulling back the corners of eyes. "Her aunt's the weirdo with the clunky bracelets. I don't know. She brought something wrapped in a little box. Probably marijuana." Mrs. Fogley's laugh sounds like a bark. "Just hurry."

Mem sits up. The washcloth falls to the floor with a thud. "I want to go home now. May I please go home?"

Wendy Fogley's dad has a long, sad face and bright blue eyes like Wendy's. He wears a gray suit and his hair sticks straight up like the bristles on a paintbrush. He smells of tobacco and after-shave. He doesn't talk much. He taps his fingers on the steering wheel, and uses his blinker when turning. "Put your seat belt on, Kiddo." He knows his safety rules. He has a small round mole on the side of his face. What if it grows and grows until it takes over his whole face?

She imagines that he comes home from work every day at five, and then he and Wendy and Mrs. Fogley eat dinner at the dining room table with all the four food groups represented. Maybe they even use flowered placemats and drink out of tall glasses of Kool-Aid with ice floating in it. She wants to ask him the story of his life, but this is not the type of thing little girls are supposed to say. She is supposed to talk about ponies and what she hopes Santa will bring her for Christmas.

Mr. Fogley hunches over the steering wheel, squinting at the houses they pass. "Do you live in Briar Park or Oak Trees?" He has a deep voice. He would be in the bass section of a singing group.

Mem searches her brain for the address. "I forget." She unrolls the window. She waves her hand against the wind, pushing it flat, then straight, then flat again. They could drive into infinity.

Mr. Fogley continues to drive slowly down the street. "Tell me when."

"There it is." She points to a two-story house with a red roof and a white gate. Mr. Fogley stops. The motor ticks as it cools.

Finally, he says, "Okay, well, you take care now."

Mem sticks out her hand. They both look at it for a second, and then Mr. Fogley shakes it. "It is a great pleasure to meet you," she says. After she hops out of the car, she stands in the driveway, waving good-bye until the red tail-lights of the car vanish over the hill.

She walks down the sidewalk, stepping on each crack. Street lamps flicker on when she goes by, like magic. In each house she passes, lights switch on, cars pull into driveways, TVs squawk, and families murmur to one other. Mem keeps walking, waiting to see something she recognizes.

She spots the house with its blue peeling paint and long shutters that look like eyes. She rings the doorbell. Marguerite appears suddenly as if she has been waiting for her return. The light from the living room lamp glows behind her, making her long hair light up. Mem thinks, Oh, Mom, even though she knows it's not her.

Marguerite's face is white and her hands flutter to the collar of her shirt when she sees Mem. Her mouth drops opens in an "oh," like someone about to sing a hymn and her features are arranged strangely, as if she's trying to decide the correct expression to wear. "Oh, honey, come in," she says, pushing open the screen door. "I have something to tell you."

Mem steps off the porch. Her fingers turn cold, like they do when she's watching a scary movie and the girl in the film moves toward a door with a monster waiting behind it.

The rule is that if you figure out just the right way to act, good things will happen to you in your life. That's the rule they teach you, but it isn't true.

Mem looks up at the sky: the dark purple streaks of the clouds, the moon a far away cold sliver, the branches of the oak trees holding the last of their green leaves before fall arrives. This next moment, she knows, she will remember.

Runaway

What he took: his entire Yankees base-ball card collection that he kept in neat rows according to team and then divided into alphabetical order. Some T-shirts, his blue high-top sneakers with his name written in blue ink on the sides and two pair of jeans stuffed into our dad's worn brown suitcase that snapped shut but didn't lock. A lucky half-dollar he found at the wax museum in Lincoln, Nebraska. His red toothbrush, an old Rand McNally road map, and his star charts. His green spiral notebooks—the ones I never got a chance to read. There must have been other things I missed or don't remember now, maybe a baby picture of the two of us, maybe one birthday card from me.

What he left behind: a blue oversized stuffed dog with glued-on felt eyes that he won playing the ring toss game at a carnival in Kearney when he was ten. His best friend Benny was with us. I threw up cotton candy after riding the Tilt-A-Whirl and Michael bought me another T-shirt to wear, one that read, "I'm with Stupid" in neon orange letters. His report cards, junior high folders, his physics books, and his yellow pencil box. Two rolls of undeveloped film still in their black canisters and an old silver Kodak camera with a broken flash, most of his clothes, his Nebraska Cornhuskers football-shaped pillow. Every dog-eared paperback book he owned, including the one he stole from the library in Springfield, Illinois. A quartz rock collection my grandmother gave him that he always hated. His microscope, his magic kit, his train set, his baseball glove that he fake-signed with Reggie Jackson's signature, a paint-by-numbers Clydesdale horse picture I made for him. A bottle of our dad's Old Spice, his bicycle, the woolen striped Indian blanket that was folded on the end of his bed for as long as I can remember. His photo album— the square pictures from Grandma's with the white frames around them, the ends curled up from age. An Easter picture of him holding me on the front steps, Michael smiling widely, my face scrunched in a toothless grin, our mother's tall shadow across the bottom of the photo. A picture of our German Shepherd, Oscar, on his chain by the barn, tongue hanging out and ears back in anticipation of being petted. Our mother's black-and-white high school photograph, a serious-looking picture of her with tight brown curls and just a touch of lipstick. All of his records including Johnny Cash, Pink Floyd, and Elvis Presley. His record player with the broken needle, his scratched up collapsible desk, Oscar's red dog collar. Our grandma's blue rosary and family Bible with our names written in her neat, cursive hand-writing, the pages thin and yellowing. A broken umbrella, his green plastic snow boots, his brown dress shoes, his leather belt, his Oakland A's baseball hat with the rim bent by his hands.

Everything, everything, everything.

Girls

One Sunday, my mother brought home a little girl. We were staying in Omaha in another of a series of barely livable apartments. This particular one remains distinct only because of a faint brown water stain on my bedroom ceiling shaped like a huge descending claw.

A week before that, she'd returned to the house after work carrying an aquarium with a jagged crack at the top. She spent the next few hours rationing pink and blue pebbles, filling the tank until the water was just below the top. I watched her float a bright yellow glow-in-the-dark castle. And then: The fish. "I got you Angels and Michael Mollies and Crystal two goldfish." She dumped the bags into the aquarium and the fish swirled and turned in frantic circles. We were used to these kinds of impulses. More than once, she returned home with stray dogs or cats. We would feed them and name them and then I'd come home from school one day, and the animal would have disappeared into thin air. That was one thing. But a little girl was something else entirely.

That afternoon, my brother Michael was bouncing a tennis ball on the side of the building, thwack, thwack, and I was inside cutting out paper dolls from the newspaper. What you did was draw a figure with a colored pencil—a big circle for the head and a long body with two arms ending in Raggedy Ann hands and two legs with patent leather shoes, then you transferred the outline to a piece of typing paper, folded it in half and cut it out— that way, you got two girls for the price of one.

The little girl's name was Crystal. My mother pulled her into the kitchen with a "Tada! We're going to take Crystal to visit her Dad in Illinois, won't that be fun?" A crust of snot covered the girl's upper lip, her hair was a clump of greasy dishwater-colored curls, and her breath piped through her nose. She had a wet cough that erupted from the deep well of her chest.

Mom took Crystal's sticky-looking hand and led her into the bathroom. "This is the tub." Crystal wiped her hand under her nose and then stuck it back into my mother's hand.

"Did she bring her own toothbrush?" I asked. Her teeth had silver caps on them. "What's wrong with her teeth?"

My mother ran her fingers under the tap water while Crystal watched, breathing loudly through her mouth. When Mom put Crystal into the tub, she just sat there, saying nothing, not even splashing. Her stomach was a fat beach ball.

After her bath, my mother dried Crystal off with my yellow duck towel. "Doesn't she know how to do that?"

My brother appeared in the doorway. "Who's this?"

Mom gathered herself together. "It's Janet's girl. I said I'd watch her until Janet gets better."

"We're taking her to Illinois." I told him, waiting to see what he said.

"In the middle of October? Do you have time?"

My mom moved Crystal's arms and legs into my Holly Hobby nightgown. Crystal said nothing, moving her arms and legs however Mom arranged them like a doll.

"We'll just take a trip and be back before you know it. Think of it as an adventure."

Michael stared at Crystal. Crystal stared back. "How old is she?"

"Can you tell us how old you are?" Mom leaned forward, smoothing Crystal's towel-wild hair.

Crystal watched my mother's mouth move. She said, "How old are I?"

"I think she's five or so." My mother led Crystal into the living room, gave her a bowl of Life cereal and sat her in front of the TV. Crystal held the spoon in her fist and scooped the cereal, leaning forward to stick it in her face and chewing with her mouth open in large gasping breaths. She watched slack-mouthed as the Road Runner ran into thin air and then, with a surprised look on his face, fell off the end of a ravine.

My mother sat behind her, fixing Crystal's hair with my soft brush, but she ducked and spilled cereal on the carpet. "Whoop-sie. It's okay."

Crystal tipped the bowl some more.

I asked, "Is she retarded?" My brother laughed.

So did Crystal.

"Jeannie, enough." My mother went into the kitchen, and Michael followed. I sat in the rocking chair, pushing it back and forth with my feet. "This is so fun." I told Crystal, even though it made me dizzy. "You're too little to sit in it, but you can when you're my age." She turned back to the TV. "Where's your

Mom?" Crystal looked toward the door as though expecting someone to walk in. "When's she coming back? Do you know? Do you have any idea?"

Crystal slept with me. She smelled like sour milk and wet dog. She coughed in her sleep and I woke up with her hot breath on my neck and her fingers circling my wrist. I peeled them off and fell back asleep, waking later to find her hand stuck to my forehead. She glowed heat and sweat. I rolled off the bed and went into Michael's room.

He wasn't there. I panicked and almost woke my mom, who was asleep in front of *The Tonight Show*, until I heard him in the kitchen.

Michael slathered peanut butter on Wonder bread and sliced it. "Who did you think made your lunches? The elves from the shoemaker story?" He cut up an apple in a half-moon, the way I liked it, and gave me a slice. "You want pickles on your sandwich?" I nodded, wondering what else he did for me that I didn't know anything about.

A few days after Crystal came to stay with us, my mother wrote a letter to our principal explaining she needed to take us out of school for a family emergency. She used the same note she'd given to the head of the last place, just retyping it to change the date. On the phone to her boss at the insurance company and also at the phone company where she worked nights, she brought a choke to her voice. "I just need a little time to deal with some things." As soon as she finished the calls, she wiped her eyes and beamed, "We're all set!"

I counted the telephone poles as they zipped by. Michael had recently taught me the secret to getting to a thousand by tens, and

I told myself that by the time I got to a thousand poles, we would be wherever it was we were going. I was sure we would crash and die, or worse, Michael and my mother would die, and I would be put in a gray orphanage, not like the ones in story-books, but a dorm with icy floors and wrought iron beds with bad springs and thin mattresses, where they served you porridge and forced you to drink coffee from a tin cup until you were addicted to the caffeine and would do whatever they told you to get more.

Michael sat in the front, a wrinkled map in front of him like a newspaper. "I think we missed the exit," he said.

My mother's voice was thin, high, like a girl's. "Oh, shoot. Well, that's okay, we'll just see where we end up after this next sign."

I sat up. "Are we lost?"

Crystal rolled over too. "Lost?"

"Yes," my mother said.

"No," Michael shook the map. "We're not lost. We're getting there as soon as you can name the capital of every state."

I lay back in the seat. I didn't like to be in the front with my mother, because she was always getting distracted by things along the way, VW bugs, billboards for wax museums, stray sneakers on the side of the road. "Now, what do you think happened to that person, Jeannie? Why would someone lose only one shoe?"

When we were nearly there, she swept into a story about Crystal's dad. She pressed on the accelerator and changed the radio stations. His name was Samuel. He lived in a cabin at the top of a bumpy hill. She had known him and Janet ("your mother," she reminded Crystal, who was asleep) since high school. They were friends of the family, had grown up in the same farm community together. She told us Samuel wrote for magazines and that they used to double date when they were younger. "I used to be Samuel's date, but then he fell in love with Janet. Isn't that always the way things go?" She found an oldie radio station she liked and turned it up. "This is the saddest! 'I'm leaving on a jet plane!'"

The bumps on the road turned my stomach. I hung my head out the window and imagined we would just keep driving and driving, until we got to a beach somewhere and then we would camp on the dusty sand and build a bonfire and tell scary stories. In the middle of the night, I'd go for a swim and meet some talking dolphins. They would take me underwater to a place no one else knew about where people could breathe even while water filled their lungs.

A man stood in the yard wearing a red-checked wooly shirt and washed-out Levis. He had wild hair all around his head. There was something different about his face, and it took me a minute to realize that he had only a beard, no moustache. He looked like pictures of Wild West men or Paul Bunyan. He grinned at us with wide white teeth.

My mother turned red.

"Look who!" He called, laughing from the bottom of his stomach.

She stepped out of the car door and he picked her up and swung her so her legs flew out. Michael slammed the door, grabbed a handful of pebbles and started pinging them onto the tin roof of the cabin. Samuel put my mother down and walked over to shake Michael's hand. My brother stepped back in surprise, but took the hand. "I'm glad you could make it. I'm going to need your help building this deck out back, if you're interested." Michael nodded. Samuel turned to my mom. "I see the family resemblance."

Around the house tall, thick trees dropped yellow and orange leaves every time the wind blew. The leaves fell in lazy spirals. One caught in my mother's hair. "You have a leaf," I told her.

Crystal stood next to the car door, her dress pulled up in the back and her hair full of Cracker Jack kernels. She had slept a hard, deep sleep for the past hour and a half, her face was lined from the seat and she looked fuzzy. I felt like kicking her for not being more excited to meet her dad. "And here's Crystal!" my mom said as though announcing what was behind door #3.

Samuel stooped to the ground. "That's a pretty dress."

"It's mine," I told him. He kept his eyes on Crystal. "How old are you now, Crystal?" She scratched a scab on her knee.

"She's five," I yelled. "She's five and I'm eight!"

Everyone looked at me. My mother put her hand on top of my head. "We're all a little tired from the road," she explained.

Samuel walked funny, sort of side to side, slinging one leg ahead and dragging the other behind, a rolling gait like a man on the deck of a ship. "You're Jeannie. With the light brown hair." He winked.

There were books and books everywhere—the only furniture besides the beds was a lumpy gray couch that took up one wall, a few wobbly chairs, and a kitchen table. "I'm in the process of building shelves." Maybe he was like my mother, never able to finish anything.

The rooms were huge with high ceilings. It smelled like bark and pine, like being inside of a forest, and our shoes made a satisfying clatter on the wooden floor. There was one big common room with an alcove for the dining room table where Samuel kept his Smith-Corona typewriter, and two bedrooms. Samuel's room had a wrought-iron bed frame and a patchwork quilt. The other room was where Crystal, my mother and I would sleep: Mom on the single bed, and Crystal and I on a larger, full-sized bed with a white chenille cover that looked like meringue. Samuel told Michael he had set up a one-man tent in the backyard. Michael pretended like he didn't care. Later, after I'd spent about an hour figuring out how Michael might get injured or killed while he was camped out back in a tent, he whispered to me, "There's no bears here, only squirrels and monkeys." He always knew what I was afraid of.

Crystal didn't act like she recognized Samuel. "That's your dad," I spelled it out in the dirt with a stick. "D-A-D." She copied me, her letters scrawling in the dry dust. She wasn't scared or excited by him. Like everything else, she took it in stride, blankly.

I spent most of the first week inventing homework from Samuel's *World Book* collection. The books were organized alphabetically and seemed to contain everything you needed to know, like what to do in case of a fire or how to perform first aid. I paged through them, inhaling the satisfying smell of glue on the glossy pages. The text was too hard to read, but you could learn a lot from just the picture captions: no one knows how stars begin or end, foxes are dogs and can climb trees, fingerprints come in whorls, loops, arches and the accidental.

Michael and Samuel worked in the afternoons building a deck on the back of the cabin. Samuel brought fresh woodsy planks and lined them up against the wall. My brother measured them with a long yellow tape that he snapped back into place with authority.

My mother began doing things she never would have done if it was just the three of us, like baking banana muffins and scrubbing the windows. "You don't have to do that, Moira," Samuel told her, but she said she was delighted to. She wore one of Samuel's red bandanas on her head and asked to borrow a button-down shirt to clean in. She started sewing curtains from an old green and yellow checked tablecloth with a foot-pedaled Singer sewing machine that whirred and gave off a pleasant, hot, oily smell. Her transformation into a more traditional Mom should have made me feel better. It was what I thought I wanted—a stay-at-home mother who didn't stumble in from work at midnight after putting in time at both jobs, and then collapse on the sofa, too tired to speak or move. Instead, her change bothered me. It was like watching an identical woman in a play step in to act the role of mother. She looked the same, but she wasn't.

One afternoon about ten days after we arrived, my mother took Samuel's round braided rugs outside, hung them on the clothesline and thumped them with a flyswatter. She gave Crystal a wooden spoon so she could help. Crystal beat and beat at the rug with a concentrated force, never coughing or stopping when the dust rose from it.

I stood next to them, worried about my fish. We left without deciding what to do with them. "We have to go back. We need to feed the fish." The thought of them made my throat ache and my stomach spin.

My mom swatted the rug.

Michael walked up, wiping sawdust on his jeans. I asked him his opinion about the fish. "They'll be okay. I gave them extra food before we left, and they can live on the stuff at the bottom of the tank for a long, long time."

"How long?"

Michael looked up at the sky and thought. "At least a couple of months, if not longer."

Mom threw down the flyswatter. "They're just fish, Jeannie." She walked inside, Crystal following her like a little dog.

Later in the afternoon, I searched under freshwater fish in the encyclopedia. I learned that they could eat plankton, but I didn't know if we had left any. I also found that to survive, sometimes the fish change colors. They blend into the background, become a stone or a part of the sand, do whatever they need to keep themselves from being gobbled up.

That night, I had the first in a series of fish nightmares that stayed with me for the better part of my childhood. The fish floated in the air outside of the tank, sucking in air and trying to find their way back into the aquarium. They were waiting for us to come back home. But the longer we stayed gone, the skinnier they grew, until the only thing left were their clean white bones.

Crystal came up behind me and wanted to play hide and seek. She'd been trailing me all morning and scared a bunch of feral cats from the shed that I was trying to lure into the house with bologna. I took her into the living room. "Fine, we'll play hide and seek." I made her promise to hide and not come out until I found her, otherwise everyone in her family would die of tuberculosis.

"Even you?" she asked.

"Especially me." I closed my eyes and started counting, and as soon as she disappeared, I went outside to see what Michael and Samuel were doing.

When I came back a few hours later, my mother had dinner ready. Samuel and my brother washed their hands in the sink and my mother asked if Crystal was still outside. I knew then that Crystal had probably fallen into the laundry chute and been killed, or tumbled into the well in the back yard. The three of them scattered outside calling for her, and I checked under beds, inside cupboards, until I found her in the back of one, eyes bright with fear. She had drawn a miniature ladder on the inside of the door with a yellow crayon. "You forget me."

"No, I didn't." I lied. "I didn't forget."

Each day, my mother became more and more like a girl, her hair hanging loose, laughing at everything we said or did. When Samuel was writing, she played jacks with us in the dirt or helped us drag the hose around to the back yard to make mud pies with stones on top in old Swanson dinner tins.

I asked Michael when we would leave. "Soon," he said. He was measuring a board with a pencil behind his ear. Being in the sun all day made him look darker, less like his regular pale self.

I leaned on his leg. "When?"

"Not long." He glanced over to my mother who was standing on the porch steps in a blue sundress, the light striking it from behind so you could see the shape of her legs through the fabric. Samuel was in the yard, putting birdseed in the holders that swung from the tree branches. We watched my mother watching him, waiting for him to finish and notice her standing there.

She stayed in the kitchen all day. I sat on the kitchen stool, handing her things, amazed at her skill. Usually, dinner was eggs or something Michael put together from a box. First, she came home with grocery bags full of red apples and vegetables— carrots, crisp celery, and small green onions. She chopped them up, humming to the radio on the windowsill. "These are my high school sweetheart songs," she said loudly, her voice carrying into the next room where Samuel tapped away on his typewriter. She was barefoot and had painted her toenails dark red. She rolled dough for a pie and baked the extra dough sprinkled with cinnamon and sugar for Crystal and me. "I'm going to take a bath!" she called again, even though we were both sitting right there.

"Okay!" I yelled back.

"Okay!" Crystal said. We set the table and I showed Crystal where to lay the silverware because she seemed to have no idea.

"Spoon!" I held it up. "Right side. Salad fork!"

Samuel stretched from his chair. "Something smells good."

Michael came in, stopping to look at the spray of Queen Anne's Lace and dandelions our mother had placed in a Campbell's tomato soup can in the center, and the white tapered candles. "I'll be in the garage," he said and left.

My mother let me braid her hair. It came out crooked, but she said, "Beautiful," and left it hanging that way down her back. Crystal thumped in the middle of the bed, squealing and singing a song Samuel taught her about people jumping off beds and bumping their heads. My mother put on lipstick and mascara and then held up her glasses. "What do you think, Jeannie? On or off?"

Without them, she looked naked. "On. You look smarter."

She nodded to me and put them back on her face. I loved it that she took my advice.

I followed her out of the room. She bent to light the candles. Samuel stood in the doorway. "This is very nice," he said. My mother laughed and pulled a bottle of wine from underneath the sink.

"Do you mind opening it?" She handed it to him and their fingers touched.

We sat down to eat. I counted the number of sips my mother had of wine, then how many glasses. Crystal chewed with her mouth open and her elbows on the table. Nobody corrected her. I started doing the same thing, smacking my lips loudly and saying, "Mmm-hmm! Good!" I tipped my chair back, rocked, holding onto the edge of the table with my fingers. Crystal copied me and fell over with a bang.

"Whoopsie-Daisy!" My mother scooped her up. "You're okay. You're not hurt."

Crystal considered this, the expression on her face changing from pain, to worry, and then nothing. "I'm not hurt," she said vaguely, reaching but not quite touching the back of her head.

The wine was finished.

My mother turned on the radio loud. "What girls want to dance with me?" Crystal jumped up from the table and hopped over to my mom like a rabbit. My mom laughed. "Very good."

"Jeannie taught me how." Crystal kept jumping.

My mother looked at me. "You want to dance, Jelly Bean?"

"No, thank you," I said, hoping she'd ask again. My mother took Crystal's hands and swayed side to side.

"You know how to jitter bug? Do like this." My mom spun barefoot on the floor. Crystal did the same, giggling. Samuel watched, finishing his glass of wine. I tried to see my mom as I imagined he did. For the first time, it occurred to me she had a whole life before I was even born. "Samuel?" Don't say it, I thought. "Will you dance with me?" I felt queasy.

Crystal had stopped jumping and was lying on the couch, her eyes droopy. I went to the sofa and pushed her to the other end. I tried to keep my eyes open, but I felt full and tired. I drifted in and out of sleepiness to that place where you hear everything but dimly, as though through closed doors—each sound muffled and dreamy and every motion in the room—footfall, vibration— reverberating through your body.

"Girls to bed." Samuel picked up Crystal first and then came back for me. I pretended to be in a deep sleep, so he would have to carry me. I let my head rest on his shoulder. He smelled like garlic from dinner and something else—an unfamiliar, smoky smell. He pulled off my shoes and socks and tucked my feet under the blankets next to Crystal. She immediately rolled over, her arm flew across my chest. I snuggled up next to her on purpose, to prove I would make a good sister. I could feel him looking at us. I kept my eyes closed though I wanted to see if he was watching only me, hoping wildly he might realize I wasn't really asleep and whisper to me how, even though I wasn't his daughter, he liked me better. Instead, he said, "Good-night, doodlebugs," and left the door half-cracked and the hall light on. I drifted off to the sound of my mom's favorite Otis Redding song, "I've Been Loving You Too Long."

The next morning, I woke to an empty bed. Crystal's high-pitched voice chattered in the next room. I sat up. My mother's bedspread was still neatly in place.

The girl sitting at the kitchen table stirred her coffee with a pen, using the other hand to try to tie her hair back in a French braid. Her hair was a jumble of marmalade colored curls like a mermaid and she wore no make-up. She saw me and smiled. She had a dimple in her cheek. "Do you want some French toast?"

Samuel stood in the kitchen next to the sink, clutching a white coffee mug in his hands and trying to smile too. "This is Sabine," he said in a loud voice. Sabine smiled at me and asked me if I had a rubber band. "My hair keeps getting into the oatmeal." I gave her a yellow one. "Thanks, Jeannie," she said. It startled me that she knew my name. Samuel peeled me an orange and let me dip it in sugar. He gave me half a cup of coffee with cream in it. Crystal perched on the end of her chair watching Sabine take small sips from her coffee cup. Crystal did the same with the juice she had, getting half of it on the front of her (my) shirt. I could see through the window beside the kitchen table that Michael was in the front yard, checking under the hood of the car. For a minute, I expected him to get in, turn on the engine, and do a slow reverse out of the dirt driveway. He looked up from his work as though he could hear my thoughts. I waved, and he squinted, and bent back over the hood.

My mother was in Samuel's bed. She was lying on her side in her slip, one arm hanging off the side. I kneeled on the floor and watched her breath come in deep sighs, like she was in the middle of a long and difficult dream. I blew on her face. She rolled over. I got into bed with her and she stirred, shifting so I could fit in beside her. We stayed that way for a long time, and I could feel that her eyes were open, and she was hearing the conversation in the room next to us, the sound of the girl's voice and Samuel's deep one behind it. "Is that Crystal's Mom?" she whispered. I said I didn't think so, but maybe it was a babysitter and Samuel was going to take us hiking?

The girl was saying how hard it was to find the turn-off in the dark, and how she had to pull over to sleep because she knew her car would roll into a ditch. "Why don't they have more lights up here?" Samuel's answer came in a low murmur. "Are you hiding out or what?" She laughed and my mother pulled herself up in one quick motion, leaving the bed shaking in her wake.

"Go have some breakfast," she told me, looking at her face in the mirror. "Go on. I'll be out in a minute." She pushed her face back with her hands, turning her head from side to side. I wanted to help her get dressed, maybe tell her to put on the jeans I liked because it made her look more normal.

"Maybe you should put on some lipstick," I suggested.

"That's a good idea," she answered, her voice bright.

My mother finally came out, her face heavily powdered and a dab of rouge on each cheek. She didn't speak to anyone, just announced in general that we were going home after breakfast.

Michael, who was sitting at the kitchen table gulping Cheerios, said, "You promised we could stay until I finished the deck."

My mom looked everywhere around the room except for at us. Samuel cleared his throat. "We could finish it by tomorrow. You don't have to go."

My mother's gaze fell on him. "No, thank you. I don't want to crowd you."

Michael pushed back from the table, the chair making a scraping sound against the wood. "Are you serious? You drag us up here for weeks and then when I want to stay, you screw it up? Perfect."

Crystal, who was standing by the window talking to herself, pointed upwards. "Rain!"

It poured all afternoon, splattering on the roof and turning the dirt road into slippery rivers of mud. Samuel went outside to the shed. Michael stayed under the eave of the overhang they'd built. Rain dripped onto the back of his neck, but he didn't flinch. He could stay angry for a long, long time.

My mother stood at the door, smoking menthol cigarettes and sticking her head out the door to look at the sky every few minutes. Our bags waited next to the hat stand. "As soon as it lets up," she told me.

Sabine pulled supplies from a black tapestry bag just like Mary Poppins—old socks, felt, yarn, Elmer's glue, and little round buttons for eyes. She called Crystal over to her and showed her how to make a sock puppet. Crystal glued everything on wrong. I stayed by the door watching.

"It's okay. Go ahead," Mom said.

It seemed I had to make a choice between doing what I wanted and what she needed me to do. "No," I said. "Sock puppets are ridiculous."

She petted my head. "How do you always know exactly what I need to hear?"

I sank into the sofa, watching Crystal's puppet take shape. She put it on her arm and climbed on the sofa next to me. "Blah!" she thrust the puppet in my face. "He likes you. Blah! Blah! Blah!"

Sabine spoke, her voice low and throaty, like a movie star. She looked younger than my mother, but sounded and acted older. "It was nice of you to bring Crystal here." My mother poked her head out of the door again. "How is Janet doing?"

"Not good." She raked the rain out of her hair.

Michael and Samuel came in. "Have you packed Crystal's things?" Samuel asked, pulling hard on the back door to shut it.

"No." My mother crossed her arms.

"We'd better get her stuff together."

"What for?" In the silence, the rooster clock on the wall tick-tocked and Crystal wrestled the two sock puppets on the ends of her hands like they were fighting or kissing.

Samuel paced forward, then retreated. "She's got to go back with you."

She laughed. "Not possible. She's your daughter. Take some responsibility for once."

Michael said, "Mom."

My mother stared at him, her face drawn and white. "What, Michael? What? You're welcome to stay here." He said nothing. "Isn't that what you want? Okay, I'm going to the car. This is bullshit." She grabbed her coat from the rack.

Samuel came over to her. "She can't stay here."

"Oh, yes, she can." She buttoned her coat. "I'm going to the car. In five minutes, I'm leaving." She said to us. She picked up her bag and slammed out the door, walking straight through the rain in even paces, without ducking or hurrying or stepping over puddles.

The idea seized me that I would never see Samuel or Crystal again, ever. I walked around the room, trying take a picture for later: the sooty fireplace, the snaky hiss the heaters made at night, the exact shape of Crystal's face. Crystal stayed still on the sofa, watching me look around, opening and shutting the mouths of the sock puppet in an absent-minded way.

"Bye," I opened the door and ran to the car, jumping in the back seat.

The windshield wipers squeaked. My mother started the car and honked the horn. "Michael's coming," I told her. My chest

went, thump-thump, thump-thump in time to the wipers. The
rain turned to hail, hitting the roof of the car with muted thuds.

I kept my hand on the door handle.

Michael stood in the cabin doorway. My mother moved her
hand as though she were going to honk again, but paused, waiting
to see what he would do.

Please, please, please. I squeezed my eyes shut and sent thought
rays to him as hard as I could, until my head throbbed with the
effort. When I opened my eyes, he was still under the eave.

Then he dodged the rain, ran toward us as though he'd like to
hurtle over the car, and then yanked open the door, sitting down
hard in the backseat next to me.

My mother didn't say anything. She just put the car in reverse.

Crystal came out on the front porch. She didn't seem to realize we were leaving. First, she was waving and waving, maybe
thinking we were going somewhere to bring back Kentucky
Fried Chicken.

But as we backed out of the driveway, her face changed. She
stopped waving. She put her hand to her mouth, her lips forming
an "oh," of surprise that gave her a strangely grown-up appearance.

My mother gripped the steering wheel and backed up slowly,
tires spinning in the mud. "Do not cry." She clamped her teeth
together. "I mean it. Think about something else."

I put my head down until my nose touched the rubbery
smelling floor of the back seat.

We slid and dipped down the hill, carried away by the rain.

Snowball

$\mathcal{T}$he night before my science project was
due, I had my head on the card table, a musty smelling volume of
Encyclopedia Britannica (S through Sn) open in front of me. The
book was something my mother picked up at a garage sale in
Jupiter, Florida, for three dollars. From this book, I could do my
project on: Saskatchewan, Scoliosis, Sneezing, Snowshoe Hares.
"What if I put food coloring in a bunch of glass jars?" I suggested
to my brother, who was watching a rerun of *The Andy Griffith
Show* on our portable black and white TV. "Does that show the
property of anything?"

"The property of procrastination," he answered. At seventeen, Michael could memorize whole paragraphs from books he'd
only read once, name how all the Saints were martyred, and point
out the constellations in the Milky Way in alphabetical order. He

kept maps of the world and the night sky, folded in a beige Army-Navy backpack with silver buckles. Sometimes, when we were driving from one place to another, he opened an atlas and pointed at random. "The Alps. Tigris-Euphrates. Cairo." Or "Andromeda. Sirius the Dog Star."

To this, our mother would intone, "The A&P. Stuckeys. Piggly Wiggly." It seemed they were arguing about something ancient, though I could never figure out what.

That spring, Michael would leave in his 1986 white VW Rabbit, with two hundred dollars Mom stashed between the pages of *I'm Okay, You're Okay*, and a leather suitcase she swore belonged to our father. Instead of a note, he taped a to-do list to the refrigerator: pay electric bill, buy vacuum, bug traps, Jeannie to dentist sometime this year, garbage out on Thursdays.

I keep the list, torn from the pages of one of his spiral notebooks, and have unfolded it so often that the paper ripped at the creases.

Michael rummaged through the closet and brought out a flimsy piece of plywood, set it on the cleared card table, and attached parallel train tracks with tiny pointed nails. He unpacked two train cars, the tracks, and the generator from his cardboard box. We moved frequently, and Michael had whittled his possessions down to a single crate of physics books, Yankees baseball cards, and an old Union Pacific train set—one of the few relics we had of our dad's. "We'll illustrate this thing we're learning about in physics—inertia." He raised one eyebrow, a trick I could only do if I held the other eyebrow in place with my hand.

I pictured GI Joe hurtling in a pink, naked blur through the air and landing at Mrs. Gustafason's feet. Instead of everyone "ohhing" and "ahhing," they would roll their eyes and one of the guys would ping a spitball at my head. "Will this be stupid?" Already, Scott Roach, a buck-tooth kid with a blond buzz cut had twice called me "Horsey Girl" because he'd seen me check out *The Secrets of Palominos* from the school library.

While Michael explained the project, I stared out the window at the rabbit hutches in our next door neighbor's back yard. The rabbits, hunkered down in the April heat, were glowing white lumps.

If the project worked, Timothy Hurst, with his broad swimmer's shoulders and freckled nose might lean against the lockers seventh period, waiting for me. He might say, "Hey, I saw your science project and I'd like to talk to you about it." We might walk home together with salty taste of humidity on our lips, and he might press my back against the spiky bark of a banyan palm tree.

Michael snapped his fingers. "Please return to planet Earth."

The objective was to illustrate that bodies in motion stay in motion unless acted on by a greater force. On the roof of one train, he secured my naked GI Joe doll with a thick rubber band. On the other train, he tied my Skipper Malibu Barbie with a length of red thread. GI Joe, he explained, would stay on when the train hit the plastic horses at the ends of each track. Skipper, with less to keep her in place, would hit the pony and fly through the air.

"Let's run a test." Michael started the engine, which blew out a gasoline smell and made chugging noises. He pushed the lever on the engine and the trains moved forward, Skipper's smile and GI Joe's clenched jaw pointing toward the cracks in the plaster ceiling. When they reached the two horses, Skipper flipped forward but didn't fall, and GI Joe did. "Well, that didn't work." Michael said, moving the trains back to the starting point. "They need to go faster."

"Could we at least find some clothes for him?" GI Joe's nakedness glowed like a lighthouse. "Won't this whole thing be nerdy?"

He stared at me. While my mother and I had the same dark blue eyes, Michael's were an odd brown. "Of course it's nerdy. Everything scientific is nerdy."

Our mother did not suffer from inertia.

"Change keeps us young!" she would yell, which meant we would soon be headed toward Punxsutawney or Birmingham or Withlacochee. Everything we owned was collapsible—the card table, the cots, even our bookshelves could be made to fit in the trunk of her Buick. "Why don't we just live in a tent?" I suggested once.

For a horrifying moment, she tilted her head back and considered it. "Because of the bugs," she decided.

When Michael discovered we were moving again, to Florida this time, he said, "Fuck." He wrote it in black marker on his sneakers—fuck, fuck, fuck. Mom pretended not to notice.

We sped down a two-lane highway in Georgia, weeping willows, cypress, and red and white oleanders bursting up from the ditches. At night, our headlights picked up the dead animal carcasses on the side of the road.

"Guess the body." Mom suggested. Sometimes, the torsos looked like they'd been flattened by a steamroller. We saw a stray dog, raccoons, armadillos, skunks, snakes, and a reddish beast that might have been a house cat or might have been a fox. I spotted a deer, for which my mother awarded me ten points. The deer lay fallen on its side without a mark, as though exhausted and just resting.

Later, our headlights caught a live deer, waiting to cross, its eyes illuminated for a second in the dark. "I hate when they stand there like that." She honked the horn. I looked out the back window of the car at the white lines disappearing on the black road. I couldn't see the deer, but I could feel it watching us go.

In Dunedin, Florida, we moved into a white crumbling apartment with a green tile roof and aqua shutters. At low tide, a decaying fish smell wafted through the screen windows. Seagulls bunched together on the roof, flinging their heads back, their white throats open to screech. If I threw bread, they swept down and grabbed it in mid-air. Beyond the seawall was the muddy black bottom of the canal. Sharp barnacles clung to the sides, quick shimmering water bugs running between them. Worse, though, were the cockroaches. My mother could not find a silver lining in the bugs that squiggled fearlessly across the floors, though she tried. "Pretend it's an alien invasion! Pretend it's us against them!"

"It is us against them," Michael said.

Michael and I took Mom's Buick to the grocery store to buy extra tacks for the project, but before we even walked through the whoosh of the automatic doors, a girl in the parking lot began flailing around, her arms over her head, like she had rolled into a hornet's nest. Her mother set down her bag of groceries and led the girl, still fluttering, to the green bench in front of the large windows of Winn Dixie.

"What's wrong with her?" I asked. Michael didn't answer. "Why is she doing that?"

We walked past. The girl trembled on the bench, her hands jerky. Her hair was cut short and her teeth protruded. A thin river of spit ran down the sides of her mouth.

The Mom sat next to her saying, "Okay, it's almost over. You did fine."

"I hope she didn't bite her tongue in half." Michael yanked a grocery cart from the bunch with a force that caused the rest of them to jingle.

"Why would she do that?" My own tongue seemed to swell at the suggestion.

"When you have a seizure, you have no control over your body. You wet your pants, chew your tongue off, or knock your head against the pavement."

I could picture having a fit in gym while Timothy Hurst stood behind me in line to climb the rope. "I know what you're thinking," Michael said.

"No, you don't."

"You're thinking, 'Will I have a seizure now? Oh, God, what if it happens in school?'" He smirked.

"I am not."

"Yes, you are. Here is a science project of the Jeannie universe." He drew a circle in the air. "Here are the rest of us, rotating around you like so many planets."

"Shut up."

"Don't worry. When you start having a fit, I'll still act like I know you. Even if you wet your pants."

Later, Pam Hammer knocked on our door. She lived in the apartment next to us, wore cut-off shorts too small for a girl of her size, had warts, and sometimes offered me her braunschweiger sandwiches at lunch.

I wanted to take her aside and give her a few key pieces of information—ditch the hats, ditch the swinging ponytail and the pigeon-toed gait, ditch the Hello Kitty lunch box, get a pair of Nikes and Gloria Vanderbilt jeans and forget about the T-shirts with bright slogans on them reading things like, "Wake me Up, Before you Go-Go." I didn't say anything though. I knew better than that.

I hissed at Michael. "Tell her I'm not home!" I hid behind our new-used collapsible hat rack.

"She's gone fishing!" he yelled.

Pam knocked again, calling, "Hello! Anybody home?" She walked in wearing short shorts and a pink sweatshirt with "Special Lady" written in cursive across the front.

She also had one of her rabbits. It wiggled. "Stop it, Snowball." She hoisted the rabbit up and tucked it under her arm like a purse. The belly of its white fur was matted and stained with what looked like tobacco juice. "Hi, there. This is Snowball." The rabbit's pink eyes stared at me with terror, seeming to silently beg for help. "Want to come over for a minute?"

"Go ahead," Michael said to me. "I'm just happy to be your servant for the rest of my entire life."

Pam's dad, in a grayish undershirt and paint-splattered jogging pants, reclined next to the air conditioner. He sat up when we came in. The apartment smelled stale, with another, more unpleasant odor underneath, like rotten cabbage.

"Hi, girls!" Mr. Hammer flapped his hand. "Don't mind me."

In Pam's room, the smell was stronger. Half-empty glasses of milk and juice littered her dresser and nightstand. The bedroom had a pink carpet, canopy bed, and shelves with Barbies still in their boxes and dolls. Everywhere else, there were rabbits—stuffed rabbits, ceramic rabbits, rabbits on pencils, posters of rabbits, a rabbit piggy bank.

"Want to hold her?" Before I could answer, Pam handed the rabbit to me. Snowball's heart pounded against my fingertips, a fast staccato hammering like a tiny drum.

"Let's go out back. There's more of them." I followed Pam out back to a small patio taken up mostly by huge wire cages. Underneath the cages were mounds and mounds of rabbit droppings that looked like tiny ruined sand castles.

Pam said, "Snowball's pregnant." She took the rabbit from me and tossed her in the cage. She immediately scurried to the back to huddle with the other two rabbits.

"Why do you have them?" I asked.

"Because they're cute." She flicked the cage with her finger. "And stupid."

"I really have to go."

"Okay, well, see you later alligator!"

The street lamps flickered on. I looked up past the grapefruit tree next to our apartment at the moon—a white glowing circle in the sky. A mullet jumped and landed with a splash in the canal behind our building and the chirring sound of cicadas crescendoed in the near dark.

Through our window, I could see Michael's head bent over the project. He leaned over to adjust another part of the tracks.

He looked up at me when I came in. "I figured out a way to make GI Joe launch off the end." He wiped his nose. The fluorescent light in the living room was too bright, illuminating the dust bunnies in the corners, the coffee stains on the table, a blush of acne across Michael's forehead.

He picked up a train car. One time, he left the train set in a Motel-6 near Atlanta. He made our mother drive three hundred miles back to find it.

It took me half an hour to dig up my earth science textbook, *The World and You.* I flipped through the pages. Chapter three was about Darwin's theory: survival of the fittest. Those who adapt live and those who don't, die.

I shaped a yellow brontosaurus from old Play-Doh. Its clay legs sunk until he looked more like a snake than a dinosaur. I stuck him in a Payless shoebox with cut-out pieces of the jungle from Michael's cast-off copies of *National Geographic.* In a second box, I glued a photograph of a smiling man from an Old Spice advertisement. Lastly, I used Mom's eyebrow tweezers to pluck a dead cockroach from behind the bathroom sink and glue it next to the man. On the dinosaur box, I made an index card that said, "Couldn't survive the cold winters."

On the other card I wrote, "Could."

By the time I finished, Michael had knocked on the bedroom door three times. "Don't you want to see how this works?"

I didn't answer.

Finally, he left me alone.

I dreamt I was being buried alive under a warm pile of bunnies. Their noses and whiskers tickled my arms. The sensation was not unpleasant. Pam Hammer and her father hovered above me, heaping more and more rabbits and whistling "I've Been Working on the Railroad." Suddenly, I was above with Pam and her dad and Michael was trapped underneath. His muffled voice rose up from below, choking on the fur. "It's a boy! It's a boy!"

The light was just creeping into the windows when I scrambled awake. My mother was still asleep in the bed across from me, wearing her work clothes from the night before.

I tip-toed past Michael's lump on the sofa. He'd left the project on the fold-out table, the two dolls lying on top of the trains like pre-op surgery patients.

Some time during the night, Michael had painted the entire board green and added brown contours, so it resembled the flat landscape of Nebraska. He had pinned a scrap of notebook paper on the front door: "Let me know if you need help carrying this in."

I tore the paper off and shoved it in my pocket. I walked over to where he was sleeping, his head crushed against the rough checkered upholstery of our Salvation Army sofa. His breathing was haggard and deep, like someone swimming against a quick current.

I carried the wood outside. I hid the trains behind the dumpster and ripped the tracks off the board. I banged the plywood against my knee again and again until it split in half and a splinter sliced my thumb. The blood welled up in a neat line like a gill. I smashed the wood again until all that was left were a few ragged pieces of wood.

The school was filled with kids setting up their projects on long tables and the hallways smelled of sour cafeteria milk and Lysol. The morning had an other-worldly quality, like something important was about to happen. I held my breath until I got to my class's row. The other kids brought flimsy posters with pencil sketches of cerebral cortexes or the food chain. There were also mobiles with multi-colored Styrofoam balls of the planets dangling from hangers and lumpy paper mache hills meant to resemble volcanoes.

I set my dioramas on the table next to Katie Bailey's poster board with crooked circles and the "Ionic Bonding: How and Why?" drawn on it.

She looked at my shoeboxes. She straightened one of dinosaur's legs. "You did it last night?" she asked. I nodded. "Yeah, me too."

Our science teacher, Mrs. Gustafason, had a brown mole the size of a nickel on her cheek, granny glasses, and short gray hair cut close to her head like a Roman soldier. It was rumored she had killed her husband by forcing him to eat the pages of an atlas.

"She's wearing her 'big girl' pants today," Scott Roach muttered in my ear. Scott sat behind me in every class, whispering pornographic and slightly thrilling things on the back of my neck when no one was looking.

"Who would like to go first?" Mrs. Gustafason spun the globe on her desk. It whirled around, a blur of blue and green and brown—there went Germany, Russia, Japan.

Pam went to the front of the room. Mr. Hammer, wearing a white T-shirt and shiny gray pants with keys attached to the belt, appeared, carrying a rabbit cage in his big hand. There was a flash of white in the bottom.

Snowball.

Mr. Hammer set the cage on Mrs. Gustafason's desk and shifted from one foot to the other. It occurred to me that not fitting in might be a genetic trait passed down from generation to generation.

Pam cleared her throat. She wore a purple dress with green balloons blossoming on it, her hair pulled back into a long stringy ponytail tied with a pink bow. She dragged Snowball out of the cage.

"This is my rabbit. She is three weeks pregnant." Pam lifted Snowball onto her hind legs. The rabbit remained still, as if stage struck. Her stomach was a little round pouch.

"Here is to illustrate her skeleton." Mr. Hammer held up the poster with rabbit bones glued on it.

Katie Bailey lifted her hand to her mouth.

Pam rested Snowball on the desk, keeping one wide palm on her snowy back, and gesturing with the other. "Rabbits can procreate between six and eight times in one year, because their gestation period is only four weeks long." An unearthly quiet descended. Not even Scott Roach shifted in his seat. Pam told us about the menstrual cycle of girl rabbits, their mating habits, the ease with which rabbits popped out babies. "Sometimes, they even eat their young," she said. Snowball tried to wiggle away and Pam flattened her to the desk. A small bead of sweat ran down her face and dangled on the end of her chin.

Mrs. Gustafason said, "A very thorough explanation. I hope Snowball has a nice big litter." Weak applause rippled through the class.

Mr. Hammer waved again and ducked out of the room.

Pam kept the rabbit cage by her feet, a small smile on her lips. I knew what she imagined: a clamor of people around her after class, begging to pet Snowball.

When I gave my presentation, mumbling about why some things lived and others died, no one said anything and Mrs.

Gustafason looked at the white clock above my head twice while I explained about Darwin and fruit flies.

Before the bell rang, Pam came over to me while I was standing at the door with Katie Bailey. She chewed on a wart on her finger. "I think we'll both get A's," she said to me.

"Your rabbit project was stupid," I told her. Her mouth dropped open, a little squeak piping out in the wake of Katie's laugh. "Leave me alone," I turned my back, furious at Pam's dumb, blank expression, like one of the faces of her bunnies.

In the parking lot, I saw Michael slumped down in his car, waiting to take me home. From a distance, he looked like a weird guy with a pale face and springy dandelion hair. "Isn't that your brother?" Katie asked, stopping to squint.

"No," I said. "I don't know who that is." Michael spotted me and raised his head.

I said good-bye to Katie and ran across the field behind the school.

Just ahead of me, Scott Roach and Timothy Hurst trailed after Pam. She moved quickly, her ponytail bobbing, lugging the cage with Snowball in it.

Scott Roach sidled up to Pam, his face cracked into a grin. "Hey, just exactly how did the rabbit get pregnant? Did you watch?" He undulated his thin hips in a slow circle, his hands over his head. Timothy doubled over, laughing. "Did your dad help you do it? Do you sleep with it at night? Are you in love with your rabbit?"

Pam turned around, her face clenched. "No," she said. "I am not in love with it." To prove her point, she opened the cage and tipped it forward. Snowball tumbled out. The rabbit stayed pressed against the grass, a white lump, stuck, not used to so much space.

The boys hooted and Scott stomped his foot near Snowball's head. Snowball jerked, but didn't run. Pam stood still, her arms folded. We both watched them chase Snowball across the grass in twitchy leaps. They pounded their sneakers near her ears whenever she paused. When they reached the thick underbrush of thorns, Snowball vanished. Scott Roach and Timothy Hurst peered through the Spanish moss hanging in blue-green clumps from the cypress trees. "Come back, Bunny!" Scott Roach called. They swatted at the branches with the stalk fan of a cabbage palm. Finally, Scott turned back to Pam. "Aw," he mugged, his mouth in a down-turned smile. "Oh, dear. I don't think he's coming back."

Pam looked at the ground. "*She*. She's a she." Pam turned to me, and then her eyes shifted back to the tangle of cypress trees.

Michael was shooting baskets in the parking lot next to our building. Sweat matted his hair to his temples. At his feet lay the broken pieces of the board and the train track. He dribbled the basketball, shot at the backboard, missed. The ball rolled away across the asphalt. He retrieved it, shot again, missed again.

"Where are the trains?" I said.

He dribbled the ball hard against the driveway. Instead of throwing it at the net again, he pitched it. It flew, bounced off the roof of Mr. Hammer's yellow Plymouth, and rolled across the yellow grass until it stopped.

My hands trembled like I was on the verge of a seizure. I said, "Aren't you a little old to be playing with trains anyway?"

Michael looked at me again. He opened and closed his mouth, but no words came out. He shook his head, got in his car, reversed, and drove away.

Good, I thought. See if I care.

He didn't leave that night; it was later. There was a headline in the *St. Pete Times* newspaper afterwards: "Local Boy Goes Missing." It didn't make sense. He wasn't a local boy.

We saw a nature show on PBS one time about the Everglades. The worst part was the alligators with their yawning mouths and black eyes slashed with thin yellow lines. Michael joked, "That's the way I want to die. Where they drown you first and then eat you limb from limb."

The police discovered his deserted car in North Carolina a month after he left. It was stuck in a ditch near a standing puddle of black water. They never found him. My mother didn't say much when she went to look at the car. She just told me there was a perfect arc of blood on the windshield. "Not a lot of blood," she said. "Only a nosebleed amount."

I pictured the tiny dried dots across the glass, like a connect-the-dots puzzle. If I could figure out which dot came first, then second, then third, maybe a picture would form: a shape like a kidney bean, Napoleon's profile, a rabbit—the same shapes we found in the clouds from the back window of the car when we were speeding on our way to someplace else.

"Was he wearing his seatbelt?" I asked her.

She lit one of her Salem lights and threw the match on the ground. "I really don't know."

In the daytime, it is sometimes enough to think that he might still be alive. The middle-of-the-night part of me knows he is not. There is no scientific explanation for this fact, but the knowledge of it wedges in my breastbone like a knot.

Once when we were little, Michael leapt suddenly from the teeter-totter we shared and I fell with a hard jolt to the playground concrete. I put my hand to my mouth. It came away red. I didn't understand how my lip could be bleeding—it hadn't even hurt when I bit it. The look of regret on Michael's face was instant, the immediate shame and jerk of his body toward me as if to take it back. "Oh, no," he said right away. "I didn't mean it."

Our Last Supper

*I*t is that last night of my sister's stay and I am determined to get her drunk. Her visit has been a complete waste of my life. I can tell she is reaching a point where she feels she must ask me something significant about my existence. There's a hesitancy about her, as if she were saying "ahem" every time she looks at me. She wants to have late-night sisterly chats in our nighties to sift through our cherished childhood remembrances until the sun peers sweetly through my mini-blinds. But when I catch sight of her, no sudden rush of love arrives. I don't think, Gee, I love my sister! Isn't life wonderful? Instead, I've spent the entire week mumbling, Dear Lord, please give me the strength not to pinch Anne blue when she bites the inside of her cheeks, which she does all day long. It's one of the many nervous habits of hers that I'd forgotten.

We're supposed to go out for farewell drinks at the Gingerman Tavern but Anne has developed a stomach-ache, caused I'm sure by the fact that she's afraid to be outside. She doesn't like the leather-jacketed teenagers loitering on the street corners and yelling, Hey, where you going? Or the broken bottles, potato chip packets, and cigarette butts lining the curbs, or any of the chaos of the city where I live.

What I hate is how Anne walks down the street with her shoulders up around her ears and how she ducks like a puppy about to be beaten when anyone raises a voice or if it looks like someone's going to get shot on TV or if an old man walks down the sidewalk with a limp. I am tired of how she has to do everything a certain way, like washing her hands with antibacterial soap or measuring out the pasta in a glass cup, holding it up to the ceiling to check the measurement before pouring it into boiling water.

And how slow she is. It takes her forty-five minutes to shower and, believe me, she is not using the scrubbie for what I do, not my sister, who calls sex "making love" and who once confessed to me she can have an orgasm by thinking about her boyfriend asking her to marry him.

Her exactness and care make me aware of my arms moving in their sockets. I have turned into an ogre lurching around the room, ready to knock a china shepherdess off the mantel with an unthinking flick of my wrist.

I make dinner on the stove, throwing spaghetti into the black pot like I do almost every night when I'm alone. I should cook some spectacular final meal with all the food groups represented, but fuck it.

Anne floats into the kitchen and opens the refrigerator door as if she's apologizing to it for needing something from inside. "If you have any lettuce, I could make a salad," she says.

I lean in next to her, our shoulders nearly touching. She smells like vanilla extract. We peer at the empty shelves. "If you can make a salad out of old grapes and yogurt." I turn back to the pasta, stirring it with a wooden spoon.

"It was just an idea." She sighs, still staring into the refrigerator. "What about bread?"

"Do you see any in there?"

"No."

"Then my guess is I don't have any."

You know what Anne is like? She's like one of those perfect girls you see in fifth-grade black and white health films from the 1950s, the kind who dab their mouths with linen napkins and wear ironed white blouses with gold buttons marching in neat rows up the front. The kind who don't slam doors and who always remember to say *please* and *thank you* and hold doors open for hunch-backed old ladies. Who carry their books tied in leather straps, swinging them over their shoulders while walking along Main Street with their boyfriends Joe or Pete who have just made Junior Varsity football and won't that be great because the girls are also cheerleaders and members of the Four-H Club. Anne was born in the wrong decade and knows it, which is why she hates the city and doesn't understand the way things work here.

For one thing, you do not take your time writing a traveler's check at the grocery store in straight blue penmanship and then spend fifteen minutes fishing out your ID and then tallying the difference in your leather checkbook. You don't count out the exact change in the middle of a bus full of passengers late for work. You are not offended when people don't say hello. You cannot expect them to be polite when their minds are filled with other things.

I trick Anne into drinking by giving her a large shot of Kahlua disguised in ice-cold milk. I tell her it will soothe her stomach. Kahlua is sweet and the drunk you get is a slow, spinning feeling like when you twist the chains on a swing tighter and tighter and then let them unravel, so the world spins and everything gets out of focus and wonderful.

I serve the drinks in big plastic cups with our last supper. Our last supper, if represented in a velvet painting like those you buy at garages sales, would show Anne as Jesus, eyes to the sky, eager to fly away but wearing a benevolent expression, hands outstretched to God. I would be Judas, lurking in the corner. The other eleven apostles would be various people in our family outlined in faint dashes, nearly invisible to the eye though still present.

Anne twirls her spaghetti on the fork. I turn on the TV and gulp down my drink to prove it isn't poison. I say, "Anne, how are you feeling now?"

She takes a small sip and sets the cup back on the table. She says, "I should pack soon." She runs her hands over her skirt, touching a thread unraveling at the hem, but doesn't yank it off.

"Yeah, maybe you should pack. We only have"—I count on my fingers—"seventeen hours until you leave." She looks at me to see if I am being mean and decides I am and doesn't say a word.

Anne came right after I told her about my conversations with Mom. I don't remember Mom very well, but one night, while I was throwing the covers around, I felt a weight at the edge of my bed, and looked up to see my mother, wearing her white nurse's uniform and smoking a Kool cigarette. I don't believe in ghosts, but there she was.

"What were Anne and I like when we were babies?" I asked her.

She said, "Oh, well, you were a perfect, perfect baby and so beautiful." She paused, her head tilted back. She had brown hair like Anne's. She looked exactly like the Kodak picture I have of her, the one where she is standing in front of Grandpa's pickup. She wears a white dress with a cabbage-sized corsage pinned on the bodice. On the back of her photo, someone has written, "Donna. Going to the dance, 1952." I imagine she had many dances on weightless feet with tall, handsome, straight-shouldered boys.

"Was Anne a good baby?" I asked my mother.

She said, "Oh, well, no, not at all. She had colic."

Anne finishes her drink.

"Do you want another one?" I ask her.

"Yes, I'll get it."

I follow her into the kitchen. She pulls out the bottle hidden underneath the sink, and splashes in more Kahlua. "Cheers," she says, holding the cup up to me.

When I called, Anne answered the phone on the second ring as if she'd been standing there for months waiting for me to call. Hearing her voice, even knowing she doesn't live where we used to anymore, I pictured her sitting at Grandpa's kitchen table, hunched over a crossword, eating popcorn in handfuls out of the big white bowl we used for Saturday night during *Alfred Hitchcock Presents.*

During the opening music, I always ran to brush my teeth and put on my nightgown so that while the show was on, I could sit cross-legged in front of the TV while Anne French-braided my hair, pulling gently at the tangles sprayed with No More Tears. I wanted so much to be the girl pictured on the bottle with the long blond hair. How could anything be wrong with her life?

I purred at the feel of the bristles across my hair, struggling to keep my eyes open. I knew if I fell asleep, I'd wake up in bed alone with one leg hanging cool off the edge. The house would be deathly quiet and a chill would ripple across my skin like a fever breaking. In those moments, I truly believed that everyone in the universe was dead and that I'd stay trapped in the purple shadows forever with the glow from the moon outside the window as the only light.

Anne switches off the lamps, leaving us in the blue glow of the TV.

She has a boyfriend now. I imagine their perfect little house sometimes when I can't sleep. I picture them living in a cottage in the woods, safe, the coffee tables stacked with *Better Homes and Gardens* magazines and fresh daisies in jars on the kitchen table. I try to imagine visiting them, but can only see myself slinking down the path to their front door in a black-hooded gown, carrying a red apple in my hand, waiting to catch Anne by surprise.

I remember one story our mother used to tell us when we were little. It was about two sisters: Snow White and Rose Red. When the good sister speaks, pearls, diamonds, and sapphires spill from her lips. When Rose Red opens her mouth to say anything, snakes, toads and spiders gush.

I sit on the bed while Anne moves from the dresser to her suitcase, carefully folding her clothes into squares and nestling each piece in her bag.

I watch her packing. "You didn't throw anything into my laundry basket, did you?"

She shakes her head.

"What about your shampoo? Don't forget your shampoo."

"You can keep it."

"No, I don't want it. I don't use that stuff." I go into the bathroom and grab the bottle. I look in the mirror, checking my eyes, my face, seeing nothing different. I walk back into the bedroom and hand her the shampoo.

"Thanks," she says, throwing it on top of her clothes.

I sit on the bed again. "We'll take a cab to the airport. The train is too slow."

"I thought you said that would cost over twenty dollars."

"Yeah, but don't worry. I'll pay for it."

"I don't mind taking the train." She says. I have to lean closer to her to hear her voice. "It's no big deal."

"Yeah, right, it's no big deal. That's why every time we ride it you look like you're about to drop dead."

Anne zips her bag shut with a sound like the end of something.

I say, "Do you mind hurrying up? I'd like to go to sleep."

She yanks the suitcase off the bed and it tips over on its side like a fallen deer.

The day I called Anne, I'd been sitting at the coffee shop, smoking a cigarette after work and watching two little girls skating in the parking lot. It was a Monday afternoon around four. Both girls had the same long, wheat-colored hair and matching purple skates. The older one could skate backwards, but the other couldn't. She held onto a parking meter. I watched her stare at her sister. Her sister was an angel, spinning and turning with her hands out to the sides and her skirt flaring. She made it look so easy.

I like the men who come to the coffee shop at seven a.m. before heading to work. I like their tired eyes and how they're still only half awake. I steam the milk and pour black coffee into child-size white cups. Some mornings, long lines form and it feels like we're in a wartime operation and I am Florence Nightingale to the rescue, let's go boys, and they are nothing but grateful for my constant attention and for remembering what they need.

Anne removes her make-up with a puff of cotton, her hair pulled back in a headband. I sit on the tub, watching her.

She is the one who taught me how to apply lipstick. She said, "Purse your lips like this." She put her hand on my chin to hold me still and brushed the lipstick against my open mouth. Her peppermint breath fanned cool across my cheeks and we both held our breath together for a minute as she finished. "There. Now blot. Never mind if there's Kleenex on your lips. Look, look in the mirror."

Anne is who I see in the mirror, her eyes opaque like the polished green surface of a fairy-tale lake.

I don't want her to leave. It's not so much that I'll miss her, it's that I don't want to find her half-moon sliver of Camay on the sink, or her hair in my brush. I don't want to watch the violets she bought wither and die in the glass jar. Her fingerprints have touched every surface and I don't want to imagine I see them some day while I'm washing dishes. I want her to vanish in the night, so I can get to the business of forgetting.

I say, "So, do I remind you of Mom at all?"

Anne looks at me. "You've got her hair. Except she used to wear it short. Short like this, to her shoulders. And you've got her eyes. Both of you have doe eyes."

"No, I don't."

"Yes, you do." Anne splashes water across her face, her eyes shut tight.

I stay on the edge of the tub, waiting for her to tell me something more.

Six Different Ways to Die in the Windy City!

ELEVATOR

In the elevator riding up to the 27th floor to work, Betsy stares at the lighted number circles that ding as they tick slowly by each floor. If she stares hard enough at the buttons, the elevator will continue upwards all the way to her floor without stopping to let anyone else on. This is the power she has. This is the way, like Atlas, she is responsible for the functions of the world.

On the 11th floor, the elevator stops with a stomach-dipping suddenness. The mail man with brown orthopedic shoes steps on. He wears a blue short-sleeved shirt and gray pants with a dark blue stripe up the middle like a high school band uniform. He nods at her and she nods back and looks at his chunky shoes.

The elevator is about the size of three upright coffins. When the mail guy leans over to hit his floor (the one right below Betsy's of course), he says, Excuse me, and Betsy presses her back against the wall. The closed elevator doors reflecting their figures make them look fuzzy and not all there.

This is the shape she remembers when he bursts through the glass doors of her office, holding a machine gun. He begins shooting. Rat-a-tat-tat. First, Maude the receptionist gets it in the back and slumps forward on the electric typewriter she uses when she's typing up envelope addresses.

Betsy ducks behind her desk. He's not looking for her. He might even let her live because of the intimate space they shared in the elevator.

His brown shoes move back and forth under the edge of her desk.

The gunfire is so fast that no one really has time to scream or scatter. His feet pivot. More rat-a-tat-tat. Someone says, Oh! The fire alarm goes off and the shrill sound almost covers the noise of the shooting. His feet vanish from view.

She hasn't peed her pants like she always worried she might do in a life-threatening situation, but neither has she done anything heroic.

The wheels of her chair spin as it's pulled back. He stands above her, shaking his head sadly as though disappointed in her.

BRACHS

She has stolen three butterscotches and two red cinnamon discs from the Jewel Osco, slipping her hand in the candy bin quickly when the vegetable kid wasn't looking. She usually takes a chewy Swedish fish or a chocolate-coated caramel, but she'd had a dream about high school the night before. The cinnamon hard candy used to be a big hit with her friends along with Devil Dog cupcakes, Dr. Pepper, and Slurpees so cold they gave you an immediate head-ache.

So she's lying on her couch watching *Law and Order Special Victims Unit* or maybe it's *Law and Order Regular Victims Unit* or one of the other *Law and Orders* that seem to be on every other night.

And it, the candy, is suddenly sucked into her air passage. It clogs her throat. She can't even breathe through her nostrils. She sits up, panicked and tries to cough it out. This can't be happening. This is ridiculous. She looks around for someone to slap her on the back. The cat stares back at her from the back of the green chair, curious.

She stands and leans over and pats herself on the back. Nothing.

Now she is wild with fear. How many seconds have passed? The inability to breathe is excruciating. She feels light-headed. She bangs her back against the plaster wall to dislodge it, knots her hands together and tries to place them under her rib cage and hitch the disc out. She was once a candy striper (isn't that ironic, a distant part of her mind thinks. She can't stop making jokes even when she's in the midst of choking). In high school health class, they were given classes on how to perform the Heimlich Maneuver on someone in a restaurant choking on a piece of steak, but your own survival was never discussed.

Nothing.

She scrambles to the door, dizzy, a gurgling choking sound from her throat, fumbles for the lock on the door, sticks her fingers into her esophagus, kicking now, jerking in desperate embarrassing spasms.

Black out. The last thing she remembers feeling is her head hitting the floor with a distant thud, and thinking briefly, I wonder what my friends will say about me when I'm gone.

WALKMAN

On the way home from the library at dusk on a regular old Monday evening, Betsy walks with her backpack loaded full of books about quirky single girls who live in major cities with their cats. She listens to Madonna's "Cherish" over and over again on her CD Walkman, imagining the mermaid in the video and the little mulatto boy Madonna swung around while singing, "I want more than just romance." She likes the soundtrack for her life that Walkman provides. That way, she can pretend to live in a perpetual movie and imagine that everything that happens to her has a purpose, is building to that last happy ending.

The perpetrator is not a Black man or a homeless man or a Black homeless man. He is one of those regular Non-Black guys with a slight criminal record of assault and battery (such as his long term girlfriend, Shelly, who finally broke up with him after he threatened to light her on fire. She went on to become a Pilates instructor and when she hears about the perpetrator on the news later, she will feel a slight rush from being a minor celebrity by association).

What makes the man move beyond the acts of giving his girl-friend an occasional broken nose to wanting to commit murder is never clear (He is caught. He is seen by a couple of high school boys walking on the other side of the street tossing a basketball between them. One, Todd, gets a good look and thinks, That guy looks like Eric Stoltz only ugly). Who knows why these things happen, but they do, every day.

Well, we may never know why, but the act was premeditated enough for him to be lurking in the alleyway near her apartment gripping a knife he ordered from a late night QVC show. He says, Miss? Miss? as Betsy passes by. I need some help. There's a dog back here that has been hit by a car. I think he might still be alive though, but maybe with a broken leg. Do you have a cell phone?

And even after having watched the terrifying abduction scene from *The Silence of the Lambs* several times and even after reading a true crime paperback on how Ted Bundy lured those nurses into his clutches, a hurt dog is another story entirely.

The man leans over between the dumpsters.

Betsy says, Oh, no, what kind of dog is it? And when the man shoves the knife in her side, she panics, wondering stupidly if the dog will be saved in the end.

Let's not go into the details. But the doctor who wrote *How We Die* was right. At moments of extreme pain, the body shoots endorphins to mask the horror and numb the brain, so that leaving the world is not as bad as you'd imagine after all.

SKY

A window washer on the 18th floor of the Sears Tower loses his balance, or a heavy piece of cement being hauled by a crane across Chicago Avenue loosens, or a sharpened icicle from the roof of Sak's thaws, or a distraught telemarketer steps onto the narrow ledge of one of those old buildings with gargoyles at the top and spreads his arms. Betsy, strolling underneath, thinking whatever it is she thinks is flattened, smashed, sliced, or crushed.

JACK LONDON

A blizzard springs up out of nowhere in a blinding haze. She can't see in front of her. The sounds of the street are lost in the shrill scream of the snow. It's not that so much as the stinging cold. The temperature must be somewhere below zero.

Betsy can't decide if she should go forward, can't see in front of her, doesn't know where the curb is. She shuffles her feet. At least she thinks she's moving her feet, but it's hard to know.

For some reason having to do with fashion, she'd forgone her winter boots, opting instead for black penny loafers and gray tights. Her feet are numb. There go at least one or two toes. And maybe her fingertips, which throb distantly in her $2.99 gloves from Walgreens. There are 3 pair of unmatched gloves in her front hallway; their companion lost wherever gloves go when they disappear, maybe to join the missing socks last seen in the dryer.

The only thing to do is to find a place out of the wind. Her hands touch brick. She feels her way to the corner of the wall, eyes shut to keep the pellets of snow away. The wind isn't quite as bad on the other side of the building.

She's freezing. What do homeless people do? Where do they go? Is there an intricate network of underground shelters?

Betsy slides down the wall and wraps the coat over her knees like a tent, keeping her back against the wall.

In fifth grade, they read Jack London's *Call of the Wild*. The boy in the book was freezing too, but he was able to send his loyal dog out into the blizzard for help. Either that or he ate the dog. Who remembers. One thing is for sure, she won't fall asleep. She'll keep her eyes open until it's safe to move again.

FLYING

The 145 Express bus, with an ad for a new Jude Law movie on one side, barrels through the tunnel from Michigan Avenue to Lake Shore Drive. This is Betsy's favorite part of the day, the momentary darkness and then the bus rising into the blinding white clear blue sky. They are flying. She grasps the pole and looks at the upturned faces in the after work silent exhaustion. They are all looking out the windows at the white strip of sand unwinding and the gray waves of Lake Michigan peaking and falling in tidal rhythm.

One of the windows of the bus is cracked open and a sharp, salty and exhaust-tinged smell comes and goes. It is a beautiful day and the crash is so fast that they don't even know it's happening, only that they're all together, hurtling forward on their way home.

Tribute to an Optometrist

 small fire has started in Thea's apartment kitchen, sparked by a second-hand coffee pot and faulty wiring. Thea stands watching it, in a moment of disbelief. The flames are pretty: blue and gold and yellow and the smell is pleasant, like a gasoline cap. It is all her fault for pulling everything she owns out of dumpsters and alleyways: a table made out of half a door and two gray cement blocks, a checkered armchair with mysterious yellow stains, a dresser without drawer handles, and this flaming silver percolator which is causing the smoke detector to shriek at 8 a.m. on a Friday morning, probably waking the entire building. Is it better or worse to put out a possible grease-related fire with water? It's like being at the optometrist, when the eye doctor puts varying lenses in front of your eyes, Better or worse? She can never tell which is better, which is worse.

Smoke winds toward the water spots on the ceiling. Thea grabs a box of Arm & Hammer and flails it in the general direction of the fire, heat singeing the underside of her arm. The flames wink out. She balances carefully on a three-legged chair and yanks the battery out of the detector. In the sudden quiet the sink drips and the refrigerator coughs off. From the wobbly chair, the cracks in the plaster walls look like they run all the way up to the ceiling and beyond, and the stove seems suddenly too small, the size of an E-Z Bake Oven. She climbs off the chair, ears still ringing from the alarm, feeling like a zombie.

Sometimes, if Thea presses her ear to the bedroom window, she can hear the woman next door on the phone with a person who isn't a very good listener. "Not Tuesday, Wednesday. No, I said 'Be specific,' not 'the Pacific.'" Last night, the neighbor spent several hours moving what sounded like a large bureau back and forth across the linoleum. Thea lies in bed, constructing possible topics of conversation between her and her neighbors. They could talk about how the dryers in the laundry room look like gargoyles, or who stole all the fire extinguishers and scrawled, "I'm going to burn this place down," on the elevator wall, or any tips the woman can give her on how to make it in Chicago, because Thea's been here two months and had not one single, interesting conversation beyond the landlord telling her not to walk too far north late at night.

As usual, Thea did not get up to ask the woman not to shout so loudly on the phone. Instead, she listened to the sound of the woman moving furniture and her TV broadcast one long car chase interspersed with things blowing up. Thea pictured it in her head, anticipating each explosion before it happened.

She leaves the mess in the kitchen for later, changes her baking soda-coated clothes, and locks the three bolts on her way out to keep robbers away from her worldly possessions. The hallway is dark and long with tall doors closed tight like rooms in a hotel. Her first week, she stumbled on a man in the staircase passed out with an empty bottle of Colt 45 by his side. She moved around him like someone skirting along a ledge, and called the police from work. It occurred to her later that she didn't even check to see if he was breathing. She worries the city will cause something to solidify in her like an icicle.

She stops at the neighbor's apartment, wondering if maybe the woman is staring out at her through the peephole, if she heard the fire alarm and is worried. "Everything's fine," she tells the door.

The wind whips around the corner with sudden ferocity, causing her to stumble forward as though a huge hand is pushing her from behind, past the Princess Funeral Home, the Egg Roll King, Manhattan Food/Liquor, the Super Coin Laundry, the Chateau Hotel, with its sign in the window, "Transients welcome." Next to the hotel is a playground with little kids running over the empty drug vials in the yellow grass. A blond girl in Sesame Street sneakers climbs the side of a gray rock with "Tina Sucks Dick" spray-painted on the side. Thea considers kidnapping the child and moving to Canada.

Among the children, Thea spots a funny looking boy on the swings. Deformities are a part of daily life now. Blind people, one-armed people, people with no legs, no teeth, missing noses; she is waiting to see a headless person wheel around the corner at any moment. This child is four or five years old, too young maybe to know something is wrong with him. Half his face is swollen like a small cantaloupe. He must have that John Merrick disease, elephantiasis. His voice carries across the yard, "Dad! Look at me! Look!" He pumps his legs in the air, pushing higher as though trying to flip all the way over the top.

A man in a gray sweatshirt and dark blue jeans turns to watch. He yells back, "Yeah, I see you. Good."

Her current theory is that everyone started in different original tribes a long time ago, but somehow, the groups got scattered across the earth like dandelion seeds. Every once in awhile, you stumble on a lost member, recognizing him or her instantly. Which explains why she keeps falling in love with strangers—an old man with a cane, a fat woman in the convenience store, this man. She stares hard at him, willing him to turn his head. He zips up his jacket and bends down to tie his shoe.

The best thing is the sound of the elevated train flying overhead like a jet, eclipsing every other noise, loud enough so you could scream along with it. From below, she watches faces of the passengers move by like a fast-forwarded video.

On her first taxi ride, the driver swerved and sped through the streets as though pursued by wild buffalo. Thea sat pressed against the back seat, watching the lights streak by the window. If we crash, we crash. There was nothing she could do except surrender. The moon kept pace through the windshield, the same one hanging above her backyard at home, where she imagined her mother standing on the porch, blowing cigarette smoke over the lawn and scratching the side of her arm like she does when she's deep in thought.

The crazy woman who loiters outside of the Sheridan El stop handing out pictures of a bloody-eyed, cheesecake-looking Jesus begins making her way toward Thea. Two bright circles of rouge blossom on her cheeks and red tangles explode around her head like firecrackers. Do not talk to me. Please, please, please. The woman says to her, "Jesus loves a giver." Thea walks to the end of the platform. The woman curses, her voice booming across the tracks, causing people to stare. It doesn't matter. You never see the same people twice anyway. "Stupid bitch, you think you're so smart because you just got laid!" She lifts up her shirt and dances across the boards, her yellowing bra exposed to the elements. "I bet you wish you could do this!" she cries. Thea looks at the gray sky, pretending she has turned invisible. The crazy woman gets closer, jiggling and yelling and grabbing at Thea's chest. She runs past the woman, nearly brushing her arm. A man in a brown overcoat calls after her, "You just met Crazy Mary."

Not one seat remains open on the bus, and everyone has decided to wear parkas today, bodies puffed out to three times their normal size, like marshmallows in fire. From the window, the gray water and brown sand mix together and unwind across the beach, and the downtown skyscrapers loom in the distance like gigantic gates. Thea sways, stuck between a woman with an easel and a man who smells like he just ate an entire loaf of garlic bread. It's hard not to notice the intimate details of other lives: cat hair on a jacket, missing buttons, shaving cuts.

The bus jerks, and the elbow of the man next to her grazes her head. The world suddenly looks murky, like everything is underwater. She blinks, realizing her contact has flown out. She closes one eye, and, amazingly, spots the tiny round disc on the knee of the man sitting in front of her. There is no room for pride in this place. Everything keeps turning upside-down. "Pardon me," she picks the contact off his pants.

"Any time," he says.

Weaving through Michigan Avenue, it's difficult not to look directly at every person who passes by, even though that is one of the things you're definitely not supposed to do. Real Chicago women stride by in thick-soled shoes with charcoal wool jackets cinched neatly at the waist, faces shut and eyes fixed on a distant point straight ahead, weaving through obstacles (homeless people, tourists) with sure-footed grace. Thea practices scowling indifferently, but catching sight of her face in a passing store window, wonders at first who that little hick is in the denim jacket. Instead of tough and aloof, she looks like she has stubbed her toe. Thea can't get the pace right, can't stop saying, Whoops, when someone gets close, can't stop making eye contact. She is waiting to see someone she recognizes, or who recognizes her.

She is twenty minutes late to the psychological intake center, where, as a temp, she is required to sit in a chair at a desk in case someone needs coffee or something. Once in awhile, she gets a stray call from a patient, but most of them are fairly normal, except for the occasional comment whirling out of nowhere like a cyclone. Once, a patient with a vaguely familiar voice said, "Oh, I think I might be on fire. Could you send reinforcements?" Thea's heart dropped like a stone. "Mom?"

Her boss peeks out of his office, eyeglasses glimmering and white hair haloed around his head like feathers. Owl. He is probably secretly tortured by her short skirts and black pantyhose. "Thea? Could I speak to you for a minute?" She brings along a yellow legal pad to show she is making an effort.

"Thea, are you happy here?" He rocks in his revolving chair, hands folded under his chin.

"I think so," she answers, clasping her knees together and fighting the impulse to swing her legs back and forth like a third-grader. The pictures on his wall shine behind his head: Stanford Doctoral degree, University of Illinois Magna Cum Laude, pictures of his wife, their golden retriever, and an aerial view of some property in Connecticut. "Yes, sir, I like it here." An air pocket percolates in her chest like a hiccup.

He swivels in his chair. His face turns bright pink when he tries to be the boss. "You seem distracted. And you're on the phone an awful lot."

"I guess I am. I have a lot of things . . ." she trails off in the middle, and they stare at the air in front of her as though both wondering what it is she means to say next. Obviously, she can't tell him about the long distance phone calls to people from her home town whom she hasn't spoken to since high school. They're always surprised to hear from her, and when she tells them she's in Chicago, she adopts a blasé tone, "At first I worried I would be raped and dismembered, but now, I hardly think about it." She doesn't tell them she chose this city because it was where her finger landed on the atlas when she decided to leave home, when everything in her mind said, Flee! Flee far away from the place where every single person knows everyone else, and where life unfolds according to an ingrained, invisible line as firm as the stream dividing the good and bad parts of town. Thea wanted something to happen, even if it was terrifying. Just something different to escape the sameness—college, marriage, babies, et cetera, death. But when they asked why she left, she said, "There's a lot of good career opportunities here," and changed the subject before they questioned exactly what her career was.

Her boss shifts, face redder, and she adds, "But I guess I assumed if you didn't need me for anything, it was okay for me to be on the phone. Was that a misconception?" Misconception is one of his favorite words, along with misrepresentation and misapprehension.

"If you don't have enough on your plate, maybe we could get you involved on one of Ginny's special projects," he suggests.

Thea nods, maintaining eye contact. "That sounds like a plan."

"I just wish you would take your job more seriously," he prompts. "I think you have a lot of potential." Oh, no, he is being kind. She can take anything but concern. It makes her feel apologetic for not working out a more effective filing system, for not staying late every day, and for not having one single, solitary goal in life. It is, after all, a temporary position. As though reading her mind, he says, "We might be able to hire you permanently, if things improve." Thea picks at her thumbnail. "Also, your skirts are too short," he finishes in a rush, as though this is the thing he most dreaded saying.

"Thank you, sir. I appreciate your candor." He sighs, relieved, and Thea stands. "Can I tell you Monday about the job?" He nods, and Thea goes back to her desk to invent new ways not to stare at the clock.

Once in a while, the people at work ask Thea what she has done over the weekend. Thea can never remember right away. "You must have been pretty out of it," says one guy, another temp, who Thea has (possibly) put on her list of people she'd like to bring home after this job is over, because he has a mole on his cheek like John Boy from *The Waltons*. The two of them could spend the winter in Montana, and she would kiss the jellybean-sized spot on his flushed cheeks when he came home from working with abused animals. But mostly, she starts rooting through the desk drawer when he walks by. So far, she has arranged all the paper clips into a chain that could stretch from the office to home and back again.

Just after lunch, John Boy stops at her desk. "Today's my last day. You coming out with us?"

Thea shuffles papers. "Oh, I wish you the best of luck in your future."

He frowns. "I won't be here on Monday."

"Yeah, I might not be either."

"Your assignment's done?" He wears a white shirt and gray pants pressed in neat pleats.

"No, but I might be leaving," she tells him. Sometimes, words fly out of her mouth like a flurry of sparrows. John Boy walks away, and Thea pinches her fingers in the drawer as penance for not knowing how to say what she means.

Sarah, the receptionist who keeps a hand mirror on her desk and always seems to be applying lip-gloss, buzzes Thea. "You have to answer this call. This woman is a nut job."

Thea looks around the office. Marsha, the clinical psych director, has taken a late lunch to prepare her bridal registry. Karen, the other intake person, seems to have disappeared, and Susan is in the bathroom, probably staring at the laugh lines around her eyes, which she told Thea she wants to have erased. Sarah buzzes again. "I'm not kidding. Just take down her information."

The woman sounds as though she is speaking through a thick wad of cotton. She says, "I can't handle it anymore." All she has are her cats and she wants to put them in the microwave. She has a butcher knife, a Volvo she'll crash into the 7–Eleven, a toaster and a bathtub full of water. She's going to jump off the top of the Sears Tower. Thea imagines what it would be like falling through space like that.

The only thing she can think to do is listen. She listens through two divorces and a kid who would rather watch *America's Most Wanted* than talk to his mother, and Jesus walking through the bedroom mirror every once in awhile. Obviously, this woman has stopped taking her meds. Thea scans the room, but no one has returned. The woman's voice tweaks higher and higher, like someone is twisting a wire in her body. Thea is reminded of primary things, the kind of questions your teacher asked in kindergarten. What do you want to be when you grow up? "Okay, what's your favorite color?"

The woman stutters to a halt. "Blue. Cobalt blue."

"I like blue. Do you have a favorite song? Like 'Blue Velvet' or 'Blue Moon' or 'Blue Christmas?'" Like everything else, she is making it up as she goes along.

"I like Elvis. I like 'Blue Suede Shoes,'" the woman says.

"Me too. I love Elvis. But I can't remember the words." The woman begins reciting them, and Thea thinks of her mom leaning across the stereo to put on records, wearing only her Sunday slip, white straps falling off her shoulders, playing the same songs over and over. Thea could recite every single Elvis track by heart. By the time the woman remembers them all, Marsha is back at her desk and takes over, efficient as a sewing needle. Thea's body flattens, the adrenaline blipping through her veins until her body gets the message. The dangerous part is over.

Outside, the air is sharp, a sign, maybe, of snow. She sidesteps people and concentrates on the blank slate of the sky, which is swept clean black, cloudless.

The subway platform is mostly deserted, except for a couple of people scattered apart, not looking at each other. A whistle sounds a low warning, and the headlights of the train barrel forward through the dark tunnel like lanterns. Thea puts her toes on the edge of the platform, just to see what it feels like. The tracks are littered with cigarette butts, candy wrappers, a diaper, crushed soda cans. She feels sweaty, like she is getting a fever.

A girl in a Michigan State jacket approaches with a map flapping in her hand. "Which one do I take to get to Wrigley Field?"

"You get on this train, here," she tells the girl. All you have to do is follow the painted signs, which clearly read North or South. The girl smiles, and Thea turns on her Walkman.

She follows a man in a brown raincoat onto the train and sits next to him, despite the empty seats. He wears a blue pinstripe suit under his coat and carries a Smith and Buckland briefcase. He looks like someone who might make you chicken noodle soup. Thea acts like she doesn't know her elbow has wandered over to touch his arm. She stares at the posters on the train. "Use condoms. HIV can be prevented." He smells like cinnamon gum and cigarette smoke. She pretends to fall asleep, letting her head tilt to the side until it rests on his shoulder. The train rocks through a tunnel and the overhead lights flicker off. Just for a minute.

He shakes her awake. "You didn't snore," he assures her, standing and folding a *Wall Street Journal* under his arm. Stocks are up. "Get some rest," he tells her, stepping off the train. The doors shut and she will not look to see if he is looking, because, of course, he is not. The train lurches forward and she turns, catching his eye as they pass each other. He mouths good-bye. "Olive juice," she mouths back.

Sometime during the day, the crazy woman from the morning has managed to find a goldfish. It swims in a bowl on the sidewalk next to where the woman sits smoking a cigarette. Thea throws the last of her change into the Styrofoam cup next to her. "That's my coffee!" Her name is Crazy Mary. "Hey, wait a minute!" Thea stops. Crazy Mary pushes herself up against the red brick wall and wobbles over. "I'm giving you this fish, goddamnit. He'll turn into a popsicle out here." Thea takes the bowl. "And this food." Crazy Mary hands her a small container slyly, like she's handing her a stash of heroin. "It's for the fish. Don't you eat it." She spits at a man walking by, "Where you going?" Thea shields the top of the bowl and ducks down the street.

One block from home, she sees blinking red and blue lights in front of her building. Thea has gotten so used to hearing sirens pass that she doesn't think about it anymore. In the dark sky above the roof, black smoke unwinds in lazy swirls. People wait on the other side of the street in various states of preparedness—some in bedroom slippers, jeans, hair wet, others looking like they have been expecting something like this to happen for a long time.

"What's going on?" she asks the closest woman, thinking, Oh, my God, I didn't get the fire all the way out this morning. "Is it burning up?"

The woman snaps a piece of gum, eyes locked on the firemen stomping in day-glo yellow coats on the front lawn. Her black hair clings against her head like a knit cap. "No, some crackhead started a fire in the lobby," she answers. "You want some gum?" Thea takes a piece of Juicy Fruit and chews it slowly. Snowflakes begin to rush sideways from the sky, as if the world has tilted.

The woman taps the fishbowl. Thea says, "Do you know any-thing about raising a fish?"

The woman doesn't ask why she's carrying the fish. Nothing fazes anyone. She blows a huge pink bubble. "Yeah, I got an aquarium. They probably all croaked dead of smoke inhalation, but I can show you what to do anyways, if you want." This must be the woman from next door. It has to be. She looks just like Thea imagined: thin, with scraggly hair, and finger tips yellowed from smoking.

Two guys in black leather jackets dribble a basketball on the sidewalk, talking in flat Chicago syllables. "The landlord is going to be up a creek come Monday," says the shorter of the two. He's got a thick neck, like a bulldog.

The other guy says, "He owes us some sort of compensation."

"Is that true?" They look at Thea, and the taller one shrugs.

"Hey, if we have to stay in a hotel, somebody's going to pay for it. And my brother-in-law works for a lawyer. He'll help us out." The short guy jogs up and down on the curb like a boxer. "If not, we'll beat the shit out of him."

Thea stops a policeman. "Can we go back inside?"

"Sure, it should be fine. Don't worry about it." The cop hands her a lollipop.

"Do I look that young?" she asks.

"No," he says, buttoning his coat. "But you don't look that old either." This sounds true, for some reason, and is a relief.

The front of her building looks like the orphanage in *Made-line* with rows of square windows, some with air-conditioners, or flower boxes hopeful for spring, curtains fashioned out of odds and ends: tablecloths, towels, a little girl's white eyelet skirt. If the landlord has to give everyone money, then it is possible Thea could afford to fly back home. She could leave behind the horse-shoe-shaped apartment building (is it pointing up or down?), the strangers shivering on the street like displaced persons waiting for soup, the smell of exhaust and the knife-sharp winter wind from Lake Michigan.

A gust bounds around the corner, lifting her scarf into the air.

What does it mean if your home almost crumbles to ashes? Is it a sign you should pack it in and give up? If the building *had* burned down, that would have been enough reason to leave.

The fish splashes, gold scales reflecting off the streetlight. This may be a sign. How do you take a goldfish on a three-hour plane ride to Florida? It's not like you can carry it in a plastic baggy or keep it on dry ice. Thea stares into the bowl, deciding what she wants it to mean.

Look at the Sky and Tell Me What You See

I'm going to a funeral, and for the occasion, I've chosen a knee-length black Donna Karan dress (Flashy Trash, $15), black lace bra and panties, garter belt, sheer black stockings and brown snow boots with my "For Funerals-Only" black pumps stuffed in a Hello Kitty backpack. If I didn't care at all what people think, I would have added purple elbow-length gloves and a hat with a dotted veil. I would've used brown eyeliner to paint a mole on one cheekbone like Marie Antoinette. I wear the garter belt in memoriam of the guy who died. He would have appreciated the effort. I also like the shiver that comes when the wind whips under my dress and tickles my bare thighs. It makes me want to squeal and bend my leg at the knee.

It's not often I can dress this way. The people at Mitch, Saunders, Mitch and Saunders are Republican lawyers whose idea of a fashion risk is a Wyle E. Coyote tie.

At the first bus stop, raincoat-wearing passengers line up at the door. I sit in the front row of seats thinking, don't you dare sit next to me. No, not you either—when this guy steps on who looks just like the man in the Levi's commercial. I beam thought rays at him. Fuck me. Fuck me now. The fat guy in front of him heaves into the seat next to mine. My man passes by, leaving a whiff of lemony cologne.

For the rest of the ride, I try out scenarios for how it could happen. The bus stalls, no—the bus driver has a diabetic fit and my Levi man takes control, yelling, I'll drive! Everyone (except me) shrieks. His manly hands grip the steering wheel. I must finish this route! I run to the front of the bus, pushing people out of my way, Excuse me, excuse me, the skirt of my dress riding up my thighs. I must help him because he's injured his left hand (it's been sprained somehow by the fat guy), and I have to steer for him, and the only way to do that is to sit on his lap.

It's too close to the premise of *Speed*, and anyway, I'd no doubt block his view and we'd crash and my mom would have to identify the body and she would be mortified to see me wearing a black lace thong.

I exit the bus at Michigan Avenue, casting one last meaningful glance at my almost-lover. He doesn't even turn his head to look at me while I stand at the crosswalk, wishing a breeze would come along and blow my hair across my cheek.

I have a minor panic attack as I enter the church foyer, because I have forgotten how to genuflect.

Then I see the guy from Divorce Law in the last pew. I usually don't find him attractive because his face is dented with pockmarks and he walks on the balls of his feet with his hands in his pockets, but when he turns, his gaze skimming over me, I notice he has the bluest, bluest eyes and you can't help but wonder what he looks like naked. Maybe underneath his starched button-up oxford he's hiding a chest rippled with muscles. Maybe he has excellent technique, very adept fingers that would make me arch my back and lose complete control, and, at our wedding, our guests would line up to congratulate us, dying to ask me what I saw in him. I would look over at his long thin, talented fingers, one now circled with a gold band, smile and say, Oh, yes, thank you for coming.

The service begins with the horn-like opening bars of "Morning Has Broken." I squeeze in next to my friend, Jennifer Sanantini, who works as a receptionist for Fred Cornell who smokes cigars and chews gum at the same time. The casket sits in the front of the church, and all you can see of the body is the tip of the nose, sticking into the air like it's testing the smell of the white orchids in large baskets on the floor.

The organ music falls silent when the priest approaches the pulpit. He is not your typical, sixty-eight-year-old holy man with a shaky voice and bald head. He's about Jesus' age when he died and he appears heterosexual. His hair springs around his head in neat whorls and he has the chiseled features like a religious figure from a stained glass window. Strong jaw, defined cheekbones, sensuous wide mouth, and sweet hands now making the sign of the Father, Son, and Holy Ghost. Holy Mary, mother of God pray for us sinners now and at the hour of our death. I want to crawl under the podium and slip between his legs while he says, Blessed art thou among women and blessed is the fruit of thy womb, Jesus. While everyone prays, he would look down at me, there, prone on my knees. He'd push my head away, his face white. For the love of God, what are you doing? I would bow my head and say, Forgive me, Father, for I am about to sin and then I would take him in my mouth and his hands would tighten on the podium and he'd whisper, No, no, you must cease and desist, but I wouldn't, and he would respond against his will.

Jennifer Sanantini is frowning at me and I realize I'm wiggling and I stop.

Sometimes, I worry that God listens to my thoughts and will answer stray fragments of them one day, causing me to be gang-raped in an alleyway by a pack of eighteen-year-old construction workers with Irish accents who resemble J. Crew models. I try to keep my prayers very explicit. Please let Jonathan Pervival Simmons from Accounting whom I know only to say hi to through Brenda Lesley in P.R. show up at my apartment one night, banging his fists on the door and shouting, Katie! Open up! I can't go another minute without touching you! This, God, must happen on a night I'm wearing my red short nightgown instead of a yellow-pitted white T-shirt and my kitty-cat flannel pajama bottom and glasses. And I have definitely not picked my face and my eyes are not puffy from crying over long-distance phone commercials and my bed is actually made, and he's wearing—but, you know, sometimes I never make it beyond the door-knocking. The details are exhausting and the struggle to make it real is too tedious and so the rest of the story doesn't seem worth the effort.

After the ceremony ends, we must file past the body and pay our last respects. I follow Jennifer Sanantini whose slip peeks under the hem of her dress. This is my first dead person in a while. I can't stop chewing my fingernails. When I finally see him, it's not that bad. He's wearing a suit I don't recognize from work. He looks the same, more or less, except it's as though his face is made of wax, like if you took a wet washcloth and rubbed a little circle on his cheek, it'd turn shiny.

A bunch of us meet up at a semi-professional bar in Lincoln Park to drink a beer in his memory.

We're there for about fifteen minutes when I spot this man at the end of the bar who reminds me of a boy I was in love with in college. Jon Preston. You had to say his full name, in whispered tones. He sewed patches on his jeans before it was even cool and I thought, Damnit! Why didn't *I* think of that? Now I can't wear patches because it'll seem like I'm copying him.

I stood in awe, every moment with him was unreal, like this gift from heaven. I'd think he didn't even know my name and then catch him staring hard at me while I was doing something stupid like trying to open the door without using my hands.

The most lucid memory I have of that time is lying on his mattress covered with dinosaur sheets. I was wearing a heavy metal square my friend gave me from Afghanistan. It hung on a leather strap around my neck. I said, Do you want me to take it off? He said, No, leave it on, and the cool gray metal thumped between us while I rocked on top of him. He looked at me with clear blue eyes, his pupils large and black with a dot of gold in the center. I wish I could draw them to show you how perfect they were and how much I wanted inside those eyes to switch places with him and know what he was seeing in me.

Three Heinekens later, this look-alike Jon Preston stands next to me. His eyes are closer together than I first thought. He says, It's loud in here. It's hard to talk.

I yell, What? As a joke. He repeats, It's loud in here. That's ten points off for not knowing how funny I am.

Then I discover he loves *Annie Hall* and he quotes the line about the raccoons and I believe we could fall in love and raise adorable children without pretentious names and move to the country and buy a golden retriever and name it Janet and in the winter, he'd wear soft flannel shirts and heavy boots and he'd chop wood and also cook oatmeal and when he'd come in from the snow carrying an armload of wood, his cheeks would be so rosy I'd want to bite them. I ask him who his favorite artist is. Norman Rockwell. What music does he listen to? Phish. What toy did he like best when he was growing up? Huh?

I say, I have to go find my friend now.

Jennifer Sanantini is listening to one of the junior lawyers tell about a messy divorce case involving a box of *Penthouse Forum* letters that the wife found to be harmful to their children. Jennifer laughs and nods and shakes her head and, when she sees I'm watching her and the guy is not, she wrinkles her nose and sticks out her tongue a little.

Our group has suddenly grown alcohol-maudlin, in part because someone put "Seasons in the Sun" on the jukebox and also because, after all, we did just come from a funeral. The junior lawyer starts telling another story, this one about the deceased and how he used to crack everyone up because he'd always forget to zip up his pants and once he walked around at a convention with the his shirt tail hanging out of his crotch. Gary, the guy who's always loitering by the water cooler, throws his head back and laughs and tries to put his arms around me but I see it coming and duck to inspect a non-existent run in my stocking.

I wonder what the dead man's family remembers about him, or maybe he lived alone in an apartment overlooking Lake Michigan. Maybe he played old Frank Sinatra records over and over and only ate Swanson pot pies. Maybe he wore checkered grandpa-pajamas and thick mule slippers and maybe he looked out the window and thought, Is this everything?

I count six baseball hats and three men in Cubs T-shirts. I search for one guy I would take home with me, just one; I have to pick one or else God will kill my entire family. There is no one. This makes me want to go home, turn off the lights, lie on the floor and listen to Counting Crows' "Omaha," even though it makes me sad because it reminds me of my grandma, whom I miss but never call.

Jennifer acts overly concerned when I tell her I'm leaving. Are you sure you'll be okay? Are you sure? Out of the corner of her eye, she's looking to see if Brad, the married guy in Damage Control, notices how good of a friend she is. Brad is not; he is guzzling a beer and involved in a serious conversation about the Bulls. I admire his leather suspenders, but only because I really, really hate them.

While hailing a taxi, I pretend I'm "That Girl." A cab zips to the curb and stops without a screech. I give the driver my address, squirming in the seat to see his dashboard ID photograph and name without him becoming suspicious.

The cabby's neck is smooth, vulnerable, and his ears stick out. Please don't talk to me, I pray. He says, It's starting to snow, huh? The wiper blades squeak across the windshield.

Yes, it is.

He says, You are coming from a party?

I press my legs together. The skin sticks. I feel like he can tell what kind of underwear I'm wearing. Maybe he can even smell me. Yeah, I say. Somebody died.

We drive the rest of the way in silence. When he pulls up to my apartment, I tip him extra for not being better company.

The snow is falling in huge white flakes, God sifting great puffs of flour from the sky. The cabbie waits to see if I make it inside okay. I want to run over to his window and say, Would you like to come up for a cup of hot chocolate? Instead, I hold out my hand and catch a snowflake on my mitten, turn, and spin for him so that my skirt flares out a little.

I look back, and he is still watching me, almost smiling. He waves and starts to drive off. I say, Thank you, and run down the sidewalk to the warmth of my building.

Words to Live By

He's confused. Too shy. His sister died of leukemia when he was thirteen. He's not over his wife yet. He's intimidated by your sarcastic sense of humor. You're smarter than he is and he can't handle it. He's lost. He doesn't know what he wants. He's never had a long-term relationship. He's young. He works too hard. He's brilliant, contemplative, needs to learn that it's okay to be vulnerable. Immature. Terrified. He needs to grow out of his Peter Pan syndrome. But you know what? She really hurt him.

Remember when he pushed your hair out of your face and tucked it behind your ear just like in the movies? And worked hard to make the perfect tuna casserole, sweat gleaming from his forehead under your kitchen light. He admired the dew on the spider webs and knew his fauna well. That one time, he said something so funny you almost peed your pants. Remember when you studied together at the Café Gourmet and you pretended to read *The Color Purple* and he was so beautiful, looking down at his book, his hand resting on his cheek, writing in the crooked left-handed way of his. He admired your Bettie Page poster.

He says your name before he comes. He's affectionate after. You both love Woody Allen films, making fun of stupid movies, sushi, Indian food. You agree you're not sure what happens when you die, but the two of you verge on hopeful atheism. He said you are the sexiest woman he'd ever met. He did the dishes without you asking. He's not bad in bed. If only he would read something besides Nietzsche or Jack Kerouac.

He's in medical, dental, law, graduate school, trying to finish his dissertation on Chaucer. He can't leave Maggie, his golden retriever, overnight. He once had major surgery. He doesn't realize he's homosexual. They moved around a lot when he was a kid. His mother was a bitch, cold, too protective, insane, unsteady, emotionally abusive, demanding, a martyr. His father made him play football when he didn't want to. He's an only child.

He taught you how to identify a deciduous tree, appreciate the artist Lempicka, comprehend Aristotelian philosophy, admire alternative country music, pick a good avocado, appreciate vintage Spiderman comic books.

His parents divorced and he still blames himself. His parents have been married for thirty-five years and he's afraid he'll settle for a love less bright or some shit. He's an Orthodox Jew. He's moving to New York in three months. He has a yet-to-be diagnosed personality disorder.

He would never hit you. He's a feminist, a vegetarian, a fallen Catholic, a poet, a canoe-maker, a yogi. He said, You're the smartest person I've ever met. He bought you a beautiful red dress and took you out to dinner and then fucked you over a chair. He knows how to talk to babies. You look prettier without make-up, he said. His life—it's too complicated right now.

You shouldn't have slept with him the first night. You shouldn't have waited. You confessed too much. You didn't tell him how you really feel. You shouldn't have said that thing.

It's not him; it's you.

The Last Dead Boyfriend

*T*wo weeks into my voluntary detox program at the Center for Drunks and Five Star Screwballs, my recently dead boyfriend shows up. I promised myself if I ever saw him again, I'd laugh in his face, Bette Davis style, perhaps make fun of his tiny penis and rapidly disappearing brown curls. I'd tell him I never loved him; in fact, I hated him more than anyone I ever met. But all my bravery vanishes with Nicholas beside me on the porch, still his same evil, beautiful self, blue eyes slanted brighter in the noon sun. I set down my crossword puzzle and put my hands on my knees to stop the shaking. What's an eight-letter word for ghoul?

He uses his husky, "take off your panties" purr. "Do you believe in the power of the dead, Mary?" Please let him be struck by a bolt of lightning, please let him spontaneously combust, because I know he is not real, I know it, but here he is in the same white T-shirt and khaki pants he wore in life, though in death, they buried him in a shiny suit he would've hated because it was not made from one-hundred percent cotton.

There's another complication—a four-month-old problem in my uterus, a DNA conglomeration of me and him, half Anti-Christ (Nicholas), half idiot (me). I can't decipher if Nicholas knows of it, or the appointment I have for what I consider the exorcism, like the fetus is a spirit that has taken up space in my body and must simply be asked to vacate the womb. A doctor on lower Wacker Avenue has agreed to suction it out. I plan on requesting a high dose of laughing gas. It hasn't moved yet, so I prefer to think of it as something that will disappear in the night without leaving a forwarding address.

Nicholas wants me to go away with him. "What are you doing here with these sickos?" We watch two kids across the street blowing bubbles on their front lawn. The bubbles shimmer like small, translucent heads. They pop in mid-air, sending soapy kisses into the grass.

"You used to be a riot," he reminds me. He is right. We had hilarious times drinking Cuervo Gold in Lincoln Park, watching the sun blossom over the skyscrapers, swaying romantically underneath the pale, star-spotted sky on those mornings when it should've been Saturday, but was really Sunday. We'd lose twenty-four hours like we'd been stricken with the amnesia that love or temporary insanity brings, assuming there's a difference.

Nicholas holds up a brown bag, the curvy shape of a bottle contoured like a body against the paper. He smells of lighter fluid and sycamore bark. I'd forgotten the sprinkle of freckles on his arms and the way his hair sticks up like chick fuzz. "Just remember how smooth it goes down." He opens the screen door like a normal, living person. He looks both ways before crossing the street, and heads toward the Blue Cat Lounge.

It's time for the mid-morning, "Confess your worst addiction stories." I tell them a story about shot-gunning six vodkas before a family reunion and throwing up through my nose during Grace. I tell them that the feeling is like the chlorine rush you get jumping in a pool, only much, much worse, because everyone pities you and tries to mop up the mess with Grandmother's embroidered napkins and they don't laugh when you ask if this means you won't be getting rhubarb pie for dessert.

The group nods and takes cautious sips of their chamomile tea.

Jeremy, the eighteen-year-old here who has been drinking alcohol since he turned twelve, rubs his five-o'clock-shadowed chin. "That sucks."

I am in love with Jeremy. He walks around picking things up and putting them down. He smells like fresh milk, like puppy breath. It's not so much that I want to have sex with him, it's more that I want to pat him on the back and say, It's okay.

During the meeting, we sit in metal folding chairs in the living room. I fantasize about getting naked with Jeremy—on the sun porch, the wooden table, on top of our head counselor's neatly made bed. I imagine Jeremy kissing me, touching the scar on my face, and running his fingers across my stomach. Nicholas' scratchy voice echoes in my head, "He doesn't think of you that way. He thinks of you like his mom. You're too old for him."

It's Jeremy's last day. Janet, our leader, has charmed him into one month of sobriety. The house we're staying in belongs to Janet, who has been sober for twenty-three years. She has potted ivies everywhere ("To keep us in good air") and no vanilla extract in the cupboards, because of the alcohol content. We're also not allowed to have nail polish remover, for the same reason. Though we're in here voluntarily, it feels less like a choice and more like atonement.

Jeremy twirls a silver half-dollar between his fingers. It's from his dead grandfather, and has the year of Jeremy's birth on it. He think it's good luck, like it could stop a bullet or dislodge a train speeding toward a damsel in distress.

Martha, one of the voluntary tipplers, clears her throat. She is sixty-five and her wrinkled face ripples with every emotion passing over it. She picks her cuticle, and pipes up in a trembling, hopeful voice, "I think it's getting better." We ponder this idea for the one-hundredth time. Yes, it must be improving, mustn't it, as though life is an escalator; sometimes you stumble, but we must all be headed to the top floor, right? Right? We nod our heads obediently and make encouraging mooing noises, pretending to give a shit.

Martha talks in a slow voice that makes you feel sleepy. Her story is hard to follow, and if you're not in the mood for it, you can sort of feel your skin begin to itch and wish you could stand up in the middle of the room and take off your pants or something to make her stop. Her tale of woe begins like all the other ones, Blah, blah, blah, my husband turned out just like his father, we don't have a good marriage, my children never come over anymore, etc., but then one day something happened. "My husband brought home a bottle of vodka and we got into a fight because he knew I was trying to quit. I poured half a glass on the floor and we drank most of the rest. Then, he left." I imagine her house, an old fashioned place with covers on the chairs and white tatted doilies on polished tables. "We were watching my daughter's baby. I fell asleep." She woke up later and it was dark and quiet and she thought for a minute that she was in her mother's house and still a little girl. She heard a commotion and realized it was the baby, hollering in the crib they'd set up in the other room. "I didn't feel like getting up, so I listened to her cry for awhile and then I remembered how my daughter used to go back to sleep if you took her for long walks." She took the baby outside, but it was snowing and icy and she dropped it headfirst on the sidewalk.

"I picked her up right away. I walked around the block with her and wrapped the blanket around her head." She laughs and then hiccups; her glasses slide down her nose.

We sit there, trying to think of something to say. There is nothing.

Somewhere upstairs, a door slams and footsteps creak across the floor.

"What do you think, Mary?" Janet asks. She looks like a sideshow exhibit for the Crocodile Lady. She has scaly skin and a large, rutabaga-shaped nose. She is one of those people who is so unattractive, you can't stop staring at her.

"I think we should have cocktails at four. A last hurrah for Jeremy." Janet tries to smile, but I can see she would like to punch me in the face.

Janet pulls me aside after the meeting and hands me a book *What to Expect When You're Expecting*. On the cover is a drawing of a snowy-white woman with a watermelon belly sitting in a rocking chair. Janet blocks the doorway. "Do you have a doctor?"

"Yes, I'm seeing one tomorrow." I try to skirt around her. She puts her hand on my arm, making me jump.

"So you're not going to have it?"

I step back. "Do I need a permission slip?"

"Is your decision based on what happened?" That's what I can't stand about this place. Janet wants us to put on little mining caps with glowing lights and explore the caverns of our subconscious mind.

I say, "Hey, I have an idea. Fuck off."

Janice purses her mouth. She squints up at the tulip-shaped kitchen light. "That's what I like most about you, Mary." She smiles at me. "You're a bitch." She pushes the book into my hand and squeaks away on her white sneakers.

The book contains helpful sketches of the fetus curled up cozily in the womb. At three months, it looks like a bigheaded tadpole with fists and eyelids. Chapter three explains how it can hear your heart beat, blood swirling through your veins, any songs you might care to sing. It cannot breathe without you. It eats what you eat, smokes what you smoke, drinks what you drink.

I sit at the kitchen table and draw tiny little horns on the fetus' head and a vaudeville mustache under its sweet little lip.

Jeremy walks in and leans over my shoulder. "Suppose it's a girl?" He has a gap between his front teeth. He smells like a saucer of cream. I guess because he's leaving, he tells me my scar doesn't look too bad.

"Does it make me mysterious?" The scar runs from my cheek down to my neck like a crack. It's from a piece of glass.

He thinks about it. "Not mysterious, but kind of like, you know, you're vulnerable or something."

I throw the book in the trash.

Jeremy fishes it out. "What will you do without me?"

"Throw a big party." I pinch his arm. "I'm getting drunk as soon as you leave, so I'll probably forget all about you."

He pouts. "That's not funny."

"Just kidding. Seriously." I cross my heart and hope to die.

Jeremy tells me about his plan to head West. His dad's out there, and even though he hasn't seen him since he was ten, it might be a good time to catch up.

I tap my foot. "Don't read any of the Beat poets on the way, because they'll make you feel like you're high, and then you'll want to get high, and I am not your mother. I will not pick your cute butt off any Sunset Strip sidewalk." Jeremy laughs, another reason I might fall in love with him. He thinks I know something he should.

We have chocolate cake to celebrate his departure. Janice makes coffee. We stare at each other, until I worry Martha will start singing "Kumbaya." Soon enough, everyone exits and it's just me and Jeremy. He licks the frosting off his fingers. "Will you write?"

"I'll send smoke signals." I scrub the countertop, sigh, look pointedly at the clock. I tell him it's past his bedtime, young man. He finally gives in and stands, stretching his arms about his sweet head.

"Have a good dream." He wavers in the doorway. I blink and smile, twirl on the linoleum, and tell him to please go away.

The Blue Cat Lounge is two turns left, one turn right. It calls to me like it misses me terribly. Using a sing-songy voice, I announce to no one in particular that I'm going for a walk.

Nicholas leans against the brick wall. In the dark, the blue and red neon cat sign winks on and off behind his head. He smokes a cigarette. His long fingernails click together. "What should we name our little bundle?" He drops the cigarette and it rolls into the curb, still glowing.

"Methuselah. Bathesheba. Lucifer. Lucy, if it's a girl, but I'm not having it." I cross my arms over my stomach.

His smiles. His canines are two sharp points. He croons, "'Having my baby. What a lovely way of sayin' how much you love me.'" He has grown skinnier and the blue lines of his veins pulse against his white skin. "I thought you always wanted a baby."

"Not Rosemary's baby." I take two steps back. The smell of spilt beer and cigarette smoke drifts from the bar along with juke-box heavy metal music, three songs for a dollar. I know exactly what it would be like to go in there.

The first drink would be the hardest because you know you're not supposed to be having it. It's also the best because it tastes familiar and good. You drink it fast, then order the second, and you get that one down quickly too and wait for the click in your brain, the one that says, What's the big deal? By the fourth drink, one side of your brain tells you you're drunk, and the other is looking forward to the next glass. You squeeze your way past a bunch of burly faced, flannel-shirted men who you don't know but who also seem like old pals. You find a bathroom that reeks of pee and sulphur and stare in the mirror, as though the face looking back at you is someone else, your mother maybe, a person who looks thwarted and disappointed in you, with a mouth that turns down and eyes that tell you nothing. You'll look at her and say, Shut up.

Nicholas opens the door to the bar. "Why not?"

I decide, for now, to say no. Nicholas shrugs and disappears inside. The tight stretch of his white T-shirt across his back as he leaves makes my palms ache and I want to follow him. I miss him suddenly, even though I never liked him much when he was alive.

I sit in front of the TV and bite my tongue to keep from crying over an old episode of *Lassie*. Timmy has gotten lost in the forest again. Lassie to the rescue! I don't even like collies. Timmy calls Lassie, "Girl? Where are you?" I despise Timmy with his cowlick and blue and white checkered shirts and big vulnerable ears. Why can't there be one show where Lassie hears Timmy calling and takes the biggest dump on the front lawn and then a long nap under a willow tree? But as usual, Lassie bounds across the cavern at the last second, saving Timmy, who hugs Lassie's big white lion mane, sobbing, "I love you, girl." I shut the TV off with my foot and go to bed.

Left side. Right side, can't sleep on my stomach anymore because of the swell of it, the fetus, baby, whatever you want to call it. I imagine it being born with one eye in the center of its forehead, gills, pushing from the womb with webbed feet, my little genetic freak of nature, reeking of whiskey and asking for a cigarette.

Or worse, it will look like Nicholas.

I go over my list of life's disgraces. What's behind this peeling door: stupid things said while drunk. Next Door: witty recoveries I should've made to stupid things said while drunk. Dumb mistakes and how I could have prevented them. Every man I've ever fucked and how that went wrong. People I no longer know.

Nicholas perches at the end of the bed. His weight is light; he's barely there. He frowns with disappointment.

The covers tangle between my legs until I push them off and tiptoe through the halls, trailing my fingers against the bumpy wall. At Jeremy's room, I stand in the doorway to see the sheet rise and fall on his chest, because sometimes after that, I can sleep.

I sit on the edge of his bed. Jeremy wakes instantly, as though he has been waiting. He finds my hand. His feels slippery. I touch his forehead. He burns hot and cold, like a kid with a fever. He's eighteen. When I was getting breasts, he was being born. He reaches for me. I take my hand away. He stops. I want him, yes.

I listen for Nicholas' voice, but he seems stuck somewhere else.

Jeremy looks at the scar on my neck. "How did this happen?"

The story I've been telling is that instead of cutting my throat horizontally, I cut down my face vertically: a dyslexic suicide attempt. Ha-Ha. "But if you must know." I lie down next to him, facing the ceiling.

What happened was this: all the movie-of-the-week elements were in place—dark, rainy night, slippery streets, too many margaritas, Nicholas driving with one hand loose on the wheel, the other pointing at me. We were arguing over the lyrics of Madonna's "Papa, Don't Preach." I knew it was "Papa Don't Preach, I'm in trouble deep," but Nicholas insisted it was "I'm a troubled sheep." I told him I never met anyone more stupid. Or more stupider. He shot me a hateful look, missed a turn, and rammed into a sycamore tree. He flew like a missile through the windshield. He survived for three days, a zombie on breathing and heart machines. Then, he died.

The doctor presented the news of his death like a joke setup. Do you want the good news or the bad news first? Your boyfriend's dead, but the good news is you're over two months pregnant with his baby!

I tell Jeremy how Nicholas knew the capital to every country, including Sierra Leone (Freetown). How he widened his eyes to scrape under his chin when he shaved. That he called my dog Fruitcake, and liked baths instead of showers. How he left things behind, mixed up with mine. A chipped blue coffee cup, the shape of his head in the pillow, a towel that still smelled like his Herbal Essence. How no matter what I thought of, it could link back to him. The Stardust Bowling Alley reminded me Nicholas never bowled. How I never really liked him, and didn't want to miss him anymore.

See, the thing is, the dead have this power, I explain, of the eternal last word. You can wave the white flag of surrender and they still linger. You can hate them, but it doesn't stop them from hanging around. I confess my fear of ghosts. I believe in them. I'm also terrified of another dead thing and what it might have to say.

Jeremy listens, breathing evenly. We're not touching, but it feels like his body radiates blue rays. I wait for his kiss, but instead, he sits up and motions for me to follow him.

We sneak out back. The wet grass crunches underneath our bare feet. Springfield fall nights are cool, but too quiet. You expect tumbleweeds to roll down the street like in an Old Western ghost town. I search the neighbors' yard for Nicholas' shape.

"I know one trick." Jeremy pulls the silver half-dollar from his T-shirt pocket.

"You sleep with it?" He nods. "You're not going to make that come out of my ear, are you?"

"No, it's a decision-making trick."

"What am I deciding?"

"It's up to you." In the moonlight, his face is shadowed and for a minute, he looks like a stranger. "Pick something." Jeremy gives me the half-dollar. "Okay, flip!" I throw the coin. It turns end over end, beautiful and slow. I catch it. "Don't look!" He clasps my arm. He has farmer's knuckles. "Now, think for a second. When it was in the air, what did you secretly want it to be? Which side were you rooting for?" I squint in the shadows, trying to memorize the curve of his mouth to remember after he's gone.

"Tails," I tell him. "Can I look?"

"Tails is the answer then." He lets go of my hand and sits in the ground.

I open my palm, just because I always, always have to see for myself.

"Is it what you wanted?"

"Yes." I move next to him, resting my hand on my stomach and listening to the katydids, a dog shouting at the moon, the wind sighing through the autumn-tipped leaves.

My stomach flutters, a slight motion, like someone blinking eyelashes on your cheek. The baby moves again, stronger, this time more like a dip on a roller coaster.

I put Jeremy's palm on the small curve under my belly button. He gets the wrong idea at first and bends toward me. "No, wait." His eyes are wide, expectant, his fingers warm against my bare skin. I search the neighbor's yard for Nicholas' shape. Something moves between the trees. I take a step back before realizing what it is: a white sheet dancing on a clothesline. Nothing more.

Wonderful Girl

*E*vie is a good daughter in some ways. When her stepfather keels over suddenly from a heart attack, she takes off two weeks from work to fly back to Iowa. She helps her mother organize the kitchen cabinet, separating the canned goods from the pasta boxes. She lets her weep and brings her Kleenex after Kleenex. She waters the plants whose leaves are brown and curling at the ends. She wears black to the funeral service, holding her mother's hand, listening to the priest drone on about her step dad and what a great man he was (as well as a dedicated Shriner) and she does not burst into hysterical laughter. She bows her head and doesn't yank her hand away even though her mother grasps it tighter and tighter as if she'll never let go, squeezing until Evie's fingers tingle and turn cold. She calls the realtor to put their cramped and unhappy house on the market. She helps her mother sort through his junk and doesn't correct her long, inaccurate, sepia-colored reminisces. "Do you want to take anything with you, honey?" her mother asks, holding up his round pocket watch, his WWII lighter, his fishing tackle box.

"No, thank you," Evie says each time in a voice like someone refusing a second serving of mashed potatoes.

She even stays to search for a place to put her mother once the house sells, but her mother, in her vague manner, finds something wrong with every potential new home.

For instance:

They cruise by Sunny Vale Retirement Village, an apartment complex made of cheery yellow brick with red shutters and flowerboxes in the windows. Reasonable rent, ceiling fans, and a weekly Yahtzee game at the clubhouse. "Oh, there is no yard!" her mother says, tapping her fingers to her lips.

"Who cares?" Her mother blinks at her rapidly like a baby bird. Every emotion she has ripples across her face, especially bewilderment and hurt. This makes Evie want to shake her or wrap her safely in a blanket. "Why do you need a yard? Will you be sunbathing?" Evie's new approach requires tough love. She's hoping her refusal to comfort her mother will force her to be more practical. But this is not how their relationship usually goes and it has put her mother out of whack. She looks at Evie like she is someone else's child, one with fangs. Evie shouldn't have been so clingy when she was younger, each separation from her mother resembling an Irish wake. She shouldn't have slept with her mother's green shirt under her pillow because she missed her so much in the night. At twelve, she should've shaved her head, gotten a nose piercing, and smoked cigarettes behind the school gym. Instead, she went to the library to check out books about misunderstood horses. She should've been a whole different person entirely.

Her mother looks out the car window. "Well, I think a garden . . ." her voice trails off, leaving a suspended silence that drives Evie to bite off her fingernails one by one.

Finally, Evie explains she really has to get back to work. Really. She has to leave. Soon. Now, if possible. She imagines dropping her mother off at the neighbor's door with a note pinned to her blouse, "Please take care of me" and speeding off into the night, like someone released from a prison sentence. Instead, she tells her mother that she has to be back in Chicago the very next morning. It's imperative.

Her mother nods her head slowly, as if she is a hearing impaired person learning to read lips. "Oh, I understand. You have things . . ."

Before she leaves, she tells her mom to call her any time, as much as she wants, day or night. Giddy with the knowledge that she will soon be gone, she even goes so far as to suggest that her mother could move to Chicago for a while. As soon as the words leave her mouth, Evie freezes, suddenly picturing her mother sitting on the sofa all day while Evie works, her hands folded in her lap, waiting patiently for her daughter to return home.

Her mother shakes her head. "Oh, no. I wouldn't think of it."

They say good-bye in the driveway next to the oil spot left by her step-dad's old wreck of a Plymouth. Her mother hugs her hard, for too long, an interminable amount of time, until Evie pushes her away. "I have to go, Mom."

"Okay, my darling." she gushes wildly, sounding like a lover.

Evie jumps in the car. She puts on her seat belt. Her mother continues to stand by the window until Evie rolls it down.

"I miss him," her mother announces. What can she miss? He was a bad husband, full of rage and given to Tennessee Williams theatrics. He liked to throw things that would shatter spectacularly. He slammed doors. When introducing Evie to others, he referred to her as "the competition." Her mother would laugh uneasily, trying to catch Evie's eye, as if telling her silently, But you know how much I love you, right? Now, her mother waits for Evie to say something, but Evie's brain is an empty cave. If she opens her mouth, bats will fly out. Instead, she rolls the window back up, puts the car in reverse, and drives away.

A wonderful girl, yes.

The phone calls start. Her mother has taken Evie's words to heart and calls at least ten times a day. Evie can let the machine pick up at home, but at work, she has to answer. Sometimes, she puts her mother on hold for half an hour at a time, hoping the theme from *The Nutcracker* playing over and over again will drive her to hang up. No such luck.

She tries to keep the calls brisk, the conversations short, and to remind her mother how busy Evie is. Busy, busy, busy. Except in real life, Evie's nights consist of crossword puzzles, braiding and re-braiding her hair, cat tricks, TV, and paint-by-numbers. So she creates a crazy social life and a complicated divorce case at work involving necrophilia. She invents a night class on wine tasting and two new best friends who have forced her to join the Chicago Social Club. She becomes part of an imaginary volleyball team that practices at the Y on Wednesday nights. She constructs such a rich and rewarding life that she begins to feel jealous of the self she's made up. When her mother exclaims about an invitation Evie has pretended to get to an art opening, Evie snaps. "Well, it won't be *that* fun."

At work one Monday morning, she suggests to her boss, Matt Becker, Esquire, that maybe it's time to change the office phone number. Ever alert in his red suspenders, MB asks, "Is someone stalking you?"

"Yes." Evie tells him. "My mother."

He steeples his hands under his chin. He is sympathetic but explains that, unfortunately, the phone number must remain the same.

"Then will you pretend to almost fire me?"

MB practices divorce and bankruptcy law. He understands the intricacies of relationships and has learned when to ask questions and when to button up. He has a second wife named Emma and a first child named Dexter and he never stares at Evie's legs when she wears short skirts. The next time Evie's mother calls, he picks up the line, speaks to her in a low, polite, and professional voice. The calls at work don't stop completely, but they slow down to once or twice per day.

Then finally one Saturday night, Evie has a real event to attend. She's been invited by a friend of an acquaintance to a party called "The Parent Trap." The idea is to dress up as a Mom or a Dad, either someone famous or one of your own parents. People in Chicago are very clever that way. She hears clever conversations everywhere: in Starbucks, on the El, in the bathroom at work. She tries to join in, but her attempts are always slightly off, like a person who has stumbled into a conversation too late and laughs before the punch line has been delivered.

The phone rings just as she's about to leave for the party. She stands in the doorway, her hand on the knob. "Evie, honey? It's me." She pauses. "Your mom." She can see her mother clearly, standing by the yellow phone, the circle of light from the kitchen lamp casting her face in shadows, half-packed boxes towering around her. "The realtor called today and said something." Another pause. "I think it was important but I couldn't find the thing to write down the phone number and so now I'm worried he's showing the house tomorrow and I just can't . . ." Evie shuts the door, locks it, and hurries away. The sound of her mother's voice echoes in her ears all the way down the long hallway.

In the elevator, she looks at her reflection in the silvery door. Her face appears distorted, as if she's under water. She surrounds her mouth with dark, dark lipstick and is startled by the results. She is all mouth. That is fine, because tonight she is someone else entirely, someone brave, a girl with an attitude.

The party is filled with Moms and Dads. There are Moms everywhere—Drag Queen Mom, a Mom with a beehive hairdo and bright pink lipstick, Martyr Mom with a fake wooden cross strapped to her back, Whistler's Mother, a girl dressed like a cat. The Dads include Mr. Cleaver, several 1950s Dads in corduroy jackets with patched elbows and unlit pipes, Dads in football jerseys with potbellies made out of sofa cushions, sitcom Dads, and a Father Christmas. Also, a man dressed as the Virgin Mary. "Get it?" he asks everyone. "Get who that makes me?"

The Moms and Dads bump into Evie who can't escape the front room. She finds herself repeating, "Oh, sorry, sorry. Whoops! Excuse me!" until finally, she's able to wrench free by elbowing a Joan Crawford Mom carrying a handful of wire hangers.

One woman in a blue dress with puffed sleeves trails around holding a martini glass between sharp red fingernails, her face covered in white powder. Evie asks the woman what her mom is like. The woman coughs neatly into her hand. "She's, like, dead." Evie takes a sip of her paper cup filled with warm pulpy orange juice and Smirnov vodka. She nods, unsure of what facial expression to wear.

The hostess Mom, with a black eye and an arm in a sling, circles around offering meatloaf, peanut butter and jelly sandwiches on Wonder Bread, juice boxes, Little Debbie cakes, and green beans.

For half the night, she is cornered by a frizzy-haired guy in a black turtleneck with a huge yellow construction paper question mark taped to his shirt. "I'm adopted," he explains. He leans in until Evie can clearly see his nostril hairs. Tiny spittle projectiles

fly when he talks. Evie considers rummaging through the hostess'
nearby dresser for sunglasses.

She doesn't know what he's talking about. Something too
intricate and personal to untangle over the music. She catches
sight of a very cute Dad leaning against the wall near the bathroom. It seems that she and the Dad are exchanging heated eye
contact, but it's hard to tell in the dim lights.

Adopted Guy has posed a question. Evie asks him to repeat
it. "I said it's an interesting idea. Do we have to turn into our
parents? You know, like no matter how hard we try and rebel and
not make the same dumb mistakes, we're sort of predestined to
fuck it up anyway?"

Evie doesn't know how to answer that question. She says,
"Oh, hold on. I think I have something in my eye." She weaves
her way over to the cute Dad, who wears a long blond wig, a tie-
dyed shirt, a suede vest with a peace emblem, and billowy-legged
blue jeans. A knot of loud-talking girls gather near him. Evie
squeezes by close enough to allow one of her breasts to brush his
arm. She feels suddenly very brave and very drunk and it's an
exhilarating feeling, as though she might cause a scene.

"Mom? Mom is that you?" Hippie Dad says, touching her arm.

Evie stops. "Son?" They're going to have the "theatre school"
conversation where they banter like two actors auditioning for
Second City. While they talk, Evie imagines their wedding, their
children, the interesting story they'll recount years later about
meeting at a parent party. He'll tell their family, "As soon as I saw
her, I knew she was the right Mom for our children."

He has straight white teeth with a slight gap in the front.
He probably drinks lots of milk. She could grow to love that
in him. "Please tell me you're not an accountant in real life,"
she says.

"No, I don't even own a brief case." It turns out he's studying
to be a geneticist at the University of Illinois. He researches the

mating habits of fruit flies. It's more interesting than one would think. Luckily, he doesn't go into detail. He has a fat, spotted mutt named Jack whose nose is flaking off at the moment. He's taking Jack to the vet very soon. He asks Evie if she likes drive-in movies. She says yes, of course, yes! The important thing is to keep the conversation going. He regrets not traveling to Prague with his best friend from undergrad when he had the chance. He takes a breath. "But wait, what do you do?"

Evie tells him about the law firm and then confesses to reading the divorce files at work. She has access to them, technically, yes, but only to fit them alphabetically into the file cabinet. But often now, when Matt Becker, Esquire, goes to court or to lunch or to the dry cleaner's, Evie waves goodbye, counts to twenty, and then opens the files to read the personal information of the clients, all written in MB's neatly blocked script, all the evidence needed for the divorce proceedings.

"What kind of evidence?" Her confession has not caused him to make a face like someone biting into a mealy apple. For this too, she might love him.

"Evidence as to why his client should get everything. Including the toothbrushes." She describes the diary the wife kept in Vituro v. Vituro. It detailed the wife's unrequited crush on the director of their church choir, and also how her husband kept old issues of *Playboy* underneath the bathroom sink, magazines their ten-year-old son could have found and been corrupted by at any time. The complaints went on for three more pages. Most files are like that, long laundry lists of small things. It's not always huge catastrophes that split people apart, not torrid affairs or child abuse or alcoholism, but something else: a slow, mundane animosity that sprouts from knowing another person too intimately for too long.

The room has thinned to only a few bedraggled Moms and Dads milling around here and there with wigs askew and smeared lipstick. The hostess flips the lights on and off. "All parents please report home to check on the children."

"I should go," Evie takes a last hard sip of red wine, hoping it hasn't turned her teeth cranberry. He nods. "Just wait for me for one second."

She ducks into the bathroom. Her face in the mirror is startling, too pale and there are dark purplish circles under the eyes. She doesn't appear glamorous; she looks frightened, as if someone has just threatened to punch her. She narrows her eyes, practices a better smile, one belonging to a starlet. She rummages through the medicine cabinet and finds a pair of scissors. She pulls down a long section of hair at the front of her head and cuts it quickly. The hair springs back, short. Now she has bangs. Or a bang. She snips a section off the other side. The two sides are uneven. She tries again. Dark hair falls into the sink in question mark shapes. Someone knocks on the door. She takes a few last hacks. She hasn't had bangs since she was twelve and there's a reason. They make her face look bare, her eyes even bigger, like a real-life replica of one of those horrible children in a Walter Keane velvet painting. The person outside pounds the door. "Hurry up or you're grounded!"

When she comes out of the bathroom, Hippie Dad has vanished into the night, lost, gone on the road with his band maybe. She knew it. She knew it. She can't pull this off. She starts for the door and nearly bumps into him as he rounds the corner with two paper cups in his hands. "Your hair!" he exclaims, taking a step back.

"Let's go," she says. She walks away without glancing back, hoping, please God, that he's following and that when she turns around, he will still be there with her. And miraculously, he is.

In the cab, Evie nods and tries to laugh at the right places as he's telling her a story about his uncle who breeds Bichon Frises. She makes a hurried mental survey of the state of her apartment as she last left it. Did she pick her underwear up off the floor after her shower? Are there neon signs of weirdness in plain sight such as the paper dolls she bought on impulse last week and cut out while listening to the audio version of *In Cold Blood* narrated by Robert Blake?

The apartment won't be too, too bad, because she's taken to keeping it presentable, due to a recent Saturday late night marathon of a true life crime series on A&E that showed colored photos of dead people's homes. They didn't reveal the bodies, but it was still deeply disturbing to witness the way some people lived, with garbage bags piled around or stacks of decade-old *People* magazines or pizza boxes, rooms that looked like the occupants had given up at some point and said, Screw it. I'll just live with the dog shit on the floor. If Evie is found murdered in her apartment, she wants the place to look presentable. She imagines the detective shaking his solemn head and saying, "What a shame that the life of such a nice, clean, well-organized girl had to come to an end such as this." It's a comforting way to live, picking up her underwear and socks, half-thinking about the detective and how impressed he'd be with her.

But now they are in front of her apartment. When Evie glances at the front of her building, she sees a fuzzy round figure sitting on the brick planter by the two doors. Her heart zigzags. Her mother! Her mother with her brown suitcase and sewing basket! But then the person moves and she sees it's not her mother at all, but the old bald man from 2-C who appears periodically to smoke cigarettes and pace along the sidewalk in the dark.

Hippie Dad seems to be waiting for Evie to speak. In the dark of the cab, his face looks young and cavernous. "Isn't that terrible?" he says.

As with Adopted Guy, Evie has lost the thread of his story. She shakes her head sympathetically. She hopes that's the response he wants. "That is a shame."

"I know. The entire face was just, like, gone."

The cabbie says, "I never trusted little dogs, " and Hippie Dad pays and they are on their way.

He walks up the stairs behind her. She jumps when he touches the small of her back as though to stop her if she starts to fall.

Once inside, they stand in the middle of the room, looking around her apartment together. She thought she was living wittily, being brave, starting over, no furniture to move besides a few things from college and an old brown sofa of her mom's. Everything else has come from the Brown Elephant thrift store or been found on sidewalks, other people's discarded furniture, including a wooden crate with "Bombay India" written in black ink on the side. She's covered it in pictures cut from magazines: a collage of children, animals, women from the 50s, a giant pair of lips, a cartoon man in a hat running from a speeding train. She has hung aprons up as curtains and nailed a rusty bicycle wheel rim to the wall for art. Now, she views her place for the first time as a stranger might. It doesn't look interesting or eclectic at all. It looks sad and desperate to please, like a performing monkey in a tiny red hat.

Hippie Dad pulls off his wig. His hair is blond and curly and beautiful. He says, "I love your apartment. It's so you." He excuses himself to go to the bathroom.

The message light on the answering machine blinks three times in rapid succession, like a warning on a heart monitor. Evie throws a dishtowel over it and then unplugs the phone and tosses it in the oven.

She's never had anyone stay over, with the exception of her ex-boyfriend from Iowa. That had been a disaster. The moment she saw his puffy, sweet face as he exited the airport terminal, she remembered why she couldn't be with him—not someone so open and vulnerable, a person too much like herself or her mother to be of much help. As a couple, they could never make a decision, always deferring to the other person. Do you want to go see that movie? I don't know. Do you? I don't know. Do you want to just rent a movie? Only if you do. They'd stumble through life together in a series of indecisive moments that left them treading water in circles around each other until both were exhausted.

After Hippie Dad emerges from the bathroom, they talk and talk and talk. They must tell each other everything, searching for some mystic parallels. Evie has to stop herself from crooning, Me too! every time he boldly claims that he loves something (the Ramones) or despises something (people who don't know how to parallel park). Love the death penalty? Me too! Hate babies? Me too! She is not herself. All of her opinions have vanished in the night like so much smoke. She's not even sure if she likes him.

It's slipping away from them, the joking flirtation from the party. They start to cover mundane topics with the utmost seriousness. The winter hasn't been so bad this year. No, it really hasn't, has it?

"Wow, this is a really interesting space." His eyes scan the room and he drums his fingers on his jeans. The more he talks, the more he slips into his dad hippie character.

She too seems to be acting more like her mother. She keeps jumping up to offer him things. Do you want chamomile tea? Are you hungry? I have cookies. Any second now, she's going to lose herself completely and bring him a stiff drink, the newspaper, and offer to give him a foot massage.

"Would you like a glass of water?" He nods. She stands, a little wobbly in her heels, and goes into the kitchen. When she turns around, he wavers in the doorway, blocking the light from the living room. Then they're kissing. "You're tall," she says during a pause.

"It's in my genetic make-up." He tugs at the collar of her dress. His mouth feels soft but not too soft, tongue wet but not too wet, and his arms around her waist urgent but not too urgent. She's becoming distracted trying to remember the fairy tale that thought reminds her of. Which makes her think of the story of Hansel and Gretel and the wicked witch. And that reminds her of the oven and the phone in her own stove, a white and secret thing, waiting.

His mouth finds her ear. "So, what's with the widow costume?" he whispers.

Evie feels her spine straighten, her fingers go cold.

When her mother called to say her step dad had died, Evie felt a stabbing pain in the palm of her hand, where she'd always felt her sharpest grief. The pain wasn't for him. She would miss him, probably, at some point, regret that they were never close, never said I love you or did any of the father-daughter things recommended by family therapists. Instead, when she heard that he was gone, she couldn't stop thinking, Mom, mom, mom. She missed her so much in that moment.

She misses her still.

Evie steps out of her shoes and kicks them across the kitchen floor. She wishes there were someone to tell her what to do next. All that matters now is that he's watching her. She'll take him to her room. She will be someone else, someone who is not afraid of the dark or of being touched by another person. She will do whatever he wants. She will be amazing. Wonderful, even. A wonderful girl, at last.

Encore

$\mathcal{I}$n fifth grade, Philip Knight asked me to go steady with him, presenting a greenish gold bracelet to me. When we broke up, he threw rocks at my bike. Bobby Dittmer wore blue All-Stars and played keyboard in a Christian rock band. I made him take the Lord's name in vain. The drama major read me a Native American prayer. Later, he stopped my hand, saying, *Why are you in such a hurry?* Patrick was the married Irish cook who declared my snow boots "dead cute." We ate popcorn by the handfuls and watched a black-and-white movie. He said, *This isn't what I thought it would be like.* Then it was. I woke up with a splinter in my back. Dan used the word "shrink," whistled Dean Martin songs, and carried a paperback by Dostoevsky in his back pocket. I didn't like him, but he knew how to push forward while on top. Jack Young wanted to hit me but didn't. The French guy poured Kahlua on my thighs and whispered, *Tonight, we concentrate on the legs.* The poet was tortured because nothing tragic had ever happened to him. Crunchy Face told me I didn't like nature enough. We watched as I stepped on an ant. Tattoo Tom wanted me to use my teeth. I traced my fingers along the green and black serpent winding around his arm. Did this hurt? *No*, he said. *None of them did.*

Katherine Anne Porter Prize in Short Fiction

The Katherine Anne Porter Prize in Short Fiction is awarded annually to a collection of publishable length consisting of a combination of short-shorts, short stories, or a novella. Selection is made by an eminent writer. The contest is partially sponsored by the University of North Texas English Department. Barbara Rodman, associate professor of English at UNT, serves as series editor. The winner receives $1,000 and publication by the University of North Texas Press.